I0582930

A Kiss to Build a Dream On

by Cora Lee

Copyright © 2024 by Cora Lee

All rights reserved. No part of this publication may be reproduced, distributed, or transmitted in any form or by any means, including photocopying, recording, or other electronic or mechanical methods without the prior written permission of the publisher, except in the case of brief quotations embodied in critical reviews and certain other noncommercial uses permitted by copyright law.

This is a work of fiction. Names, characters, businesses, places, events, and incidents are either the products of the author's imagination or used in a fictitious manner.

No part of this book was created with the use of AI. It is was produced through the hard work and creativity of the author, editor, and cover designer.

Editing by Jude Simms.

Cover by Erin Dameron-Hill at EDH Professionals.

ISBN 978-1-944477-31-8

Published in the United States by More Than Words Press

Chapter 1

The Cotswolds
July 1815

Margaret Maitland sat at her brother's dining table, as she did at least once every week, wondering how she got to this point and where she was going from here.

Not literally how she got there—she walked from the dower house, as usual—but she'd had a letter from her son, Alex, earlier in the day which sent a contemplative wave washing over her. He'd been so small when they'd first moved into that house, and she'd been so vulnerable. But he was a tall, strapping lad now, looking forward to the end of the Easter Term at Cambridge when he could come home and have some fun. Where had the time gone?

"Margaret?"

Margaret's brother Philip, seated next to her, poked her discreetly under the table. "Hmm?" she asked, turning her head toward the sound of her name.

Philip's wife Adeleine frowned across the table and set down her knife with a clank. "I asked if you and Alexander would be attending Natalie's practice ball."

"Yes, of course we will," Margaret answered readily. Adeleine had been hosting a series of informal events over the past several months to give her daughter the opportunity to practice being out in society before her first season in London. Only family and close friends had been invited thus far, but this "practice ball," as Adeleine had been calling it, would be something of a larger affair.

Adeleine's face relaxed and she sat back a bit in her chair. "Good. Natalie has been looking forward to dancing with her cousin."

Margaret chuckled, and Mr. Stephen Eddington, the Maitlands' neighbor sitting across the table from her, lifted a sandy eyebrow in inquiry. "When she was still in leading strings, Natalie decided that Alex was her favorite person in the world, and she's never wavered from that opinion."

"Ah," Mr. Eddington replied with a smile and a nod. "And Alex must return the sentiment, given how much my nephew Patrick includes her in his letters."

Adeleine glanced from Mr. Eddington to her husband, a range of emotions playing out on her face. When outrage made an appearance, Margaret caught Adeleine's eye and shook her head slightly.

"Mr. Eddington's nephew is Alex's closest friend," Margaret reminded her gently. "It's natural that they would speak to each other of the people they care for."

"Yes, that is it exactly," Mr. Eddington added. "Patrick says he feels as if he knows Miss Natalie because Alex speaks of her so often, and so highly."

Adeleine's eyes bored into Margaret's for a long moment. Margaret could practically see her sister-in-law's thoughts—she was afraid her daughter was going to be ruined before she even had a single season. Like her aunt.

Though, to be fair, Margaret had enjoyed three seasons before she had been ruined.

Adeleine nodded faintly, then smiled brightly at Mr. Eddington. "That is good to hear. And oh! Perhaps you would consider attending Natalie's practice ball as well? It will be held right here in our music room in a month's time."

"I would be honored," he replied, his hand going to his chest. "And on the subject of invitations, I came to dinner tonight with my own." His blue eyes slid from Adeleine to Margaret, and a small smile formed on his lips.

"Oh?" Margaret said, taking a sip of sweet red wine, the tide of her contemplation ebbing as a warmer wave washed in.

He grinned, then stifled the expression and cleared his throat. "For all of you. My sister and her children are coming to stay with me for several weeks, and I was hoping to persuade the three of you, along with Miss Natalie and Alex, to join us."

"Like a house party?" Margaret asked, carefully setting her glass on the table.

"A small one," Mr. Eddington acknowledged. "It would just be our two families. I've written to my friend James Fitzsimmons and your cousin Lady Cecilia to invite them as well, but I believe they are otherwise occupied."

Margaret grinned, slicing her roasted chicken and savoring the salty, meaty aroma. Cecilia had recently wed Mr. Fitzsimmons in what was supposed to be a marriage of convenience, but it had turned into a genuine love match. They were spending the summer visiting family and enjoying their new life together.

"My sister has five children, and the oldest girl is about Miss Natalie's age," Mr. Eddington continued over the clinking of silverware against plates. "Since Alex is already friends with my eldest nephew, we thought perhaps the younger ones would enjoy spending some time together while we of a certain age enjoy each other's company."

"That sounds like a capital idea," Philip said, brandishing his fork with enthusiasm. "I don't believe we'll be able to stay, not with all the preparations we must make before we travel to London after the practice ball. But your home is an easy ride, particularly when the weather is fine, and we may be able to join you some days."

Adeleine was smiling as well, but the warmth had begun to seep out of Margaret's body. "I– I'm not sure—"

"My sister has asked for you especially, Miss Maitland," Mr. Eddington replied before she could finish her thought, his voice softer now as he pinned Margaret with his gaze once again. "She wants to meet the mother of her son's best friend."

"Oh, of– of course... And I would be pleased to meet her as well..."

Mr. Eddington smiled broadly. If he heard the hesitation in Margaret's voice, he ignored it. "Wonderful! My sister will be the hostess, of course, and she'll send round the details when she arrives next week."

He turned back to his plate, fairly beaming at his food and, alternately, his companions for the duration of the meal. Margaret found the previously delicious fare chewy and tasteless, and only picked at her entree until they left the table for the drawing room. She tried to focus on the conversations going on around her, but had no luck there either.

When finally Mr. Eddington decided to return home, Margaret jumped up from her chair. "I should also take my leave."

"I'll see you to the gate if I may," he replied, catching her eye.

Margaret nodded her assent. This was their custom if they both happened to be dining with Philip and Adeleine, and it was interesting that he still asked after nearly a year of acquaintance rather than just assuming.

What was he going to say when she refused his invitation?

Neither of them spoke as they made their way through the house and out onto the long drive awash in the reds and oranges of the setting sun. But three steps from the house, she couldn't keep it in any longer.

"Mr. Eddington, are you certain about inviting me to your home, to meet your sister?" she asked, laying a hand on his arm to stop him. A lone songbird serenaded them from a nearby tree as if he had no cares in the world.

"Of course I am," he replied quickly. His brows crowded down low over his eyes. "Why would you ask me that?"

She pressed her lips together, trying to discern just the right words to convey the absolute inappropriateness of her presence in a respectable home. "You know that I raised my son without the help of his father."

Mr. Eddington nodded slowly. "Yes."

"And you also know why."

He nodded again, glancing at her feet for a moment before meeting her eyes once again. Not long after they first met, Margaret had outlined the bare bones of the story—how she had become pregnant without being married and, rather than hide her condition and give the baby to another family to raise, she had elected to keep him, to raise him herself.

It had destroyed her reputation, of course. And though there were a select few people who would now receive her privately in their homes all these years later, Margaret was still not welcome at even the most obscure society functions.

Margaret's voice was rough when she spoke again. "I truly would like to meet your sister, but I am afraid that even after twenty years my reputation would tarnish hers."

"And, in turn, my nieces' reputations as well," he added quietly.

Margaret turned and began to walk down the drive, clasping her hands together behind her back to keep from taking his arm as she often did. She wanted to, but it didn't feel like the right thing to do at this moment. "Exactly so."

"What about your own niece?" he asked, falling into step beside her. He, too, refrained from touching her, which was both a relief and a disappointment somehow. "Does she not suffer from your connection?"

"It's easier for people to overlook a rogue family member when the Duke of Alston is her cousin."

"Mmm. I suppose it's the same for your son as well."

She kicked a small rock to the side. "The stigma is a bit less because he's a man, but yes. Influential relatives outweigh a fallen mother for him some of the time."

They walked along in silence down the length of the drive, accompanied only by the rhythmic crunching of gravel beneath their feet, and Margaret felt some of the tension in her shoulders easing. She feared that she would have to explain to him the details of her situation to make him understand how bad it had been for the family and friends that had supported her, that still supported her.

But he didn't protest any further. When they arrived at the gate, he tipped his hat to her as he always did and held the gate open for her to pass through.

"Good evening, Miss Maitland," he said. His voice was even, and he met her eyes, so perhaps there were no hard feelings.

"Good evening, Mr. Eddington."

A week later later, Stephen rode back to Philip Maitland's home, Eastwood Manor, with two things in his saddle bag: his copy of *Observations on the Theory and Practice of Landscape Gardening* that he'd promised to lend to Philip, and a note for Miss Margaret Maitland from his sister, who was more than a little disappointed to hear that Miss Maitland had turned down the house party invitation.

Hopefully, both things would be well received.

"Eddington—what a nice surprise," Philip said, rising as Stephen was shown into the library by the Maitlands' butler. "Adeleine was wondering earlier about your house party activities, and here you are to ask."

"Ah yes," Stephen replied, taking his usual seat in a sturdy walnut chair. "My sister arrived yesterday with her children, and she is writing up a list. Everything is to be rather informal, but she'll send the details round when she's sorted it all out."

"Excellent," Philip answered, taking his own seat in a chair that had begun its life as the twin of Stephen's but had seen much more wear. "You must thank her for thinking of us, and of Natalie in particular."

"I will do that." Stephen fished around in his inner coat pocket and came up with the note he'd been tasked with delivering. "She also sent along a note for your own sister. Will you pass it along to her the next time she's here?"

Philip waved the note away. "You can give it to her yourself before you depart. She's with

Adeleine now walking in the gardens, but they should be returning soon for luncheon."

"Oh." Well, that was unexpected. Though Stephen supposed it shouldn't be—Miss Maitland was frequently here when he was. "Well, that's perfect timing, then. Perhaps I can take an answer home with me today."

Their conversation drifted to other topics, including the book Stephen had brought, and an hour or so later Mrs. Maitland bustled in with a bright smile for her husband.

"I hope you're hungry," she said, touching his shoulder lightly. "Our cook has been experimenting with some new recipes, and there's a mountain of food. You'll stay and taste them all, won't you Mr. Eddington?"

Stephen pulled his gold pocket watch from the custom pocket in his waistcoat. "I'm afraid I cannot, Mrs. Maitland," he answered with real regret. The Maitlands' cook always created the most delicious dishes. "I promised my sister that I would help her with a few things this afternoon. I really only came by to give this note to your sister-in-law."

He produced the note again with Miss Maitland's name written in flowing script on the outside, and Mrs. Maitland nodded.

"Margaret stayed a few more minutes in the garden nearest the house. You can deliver your sister's note to her there if you'd like."

Wonderful—perhaps she could spare a moment to speak with him, too, away from any listening ears. "I believe I will do that. Thank you," Stephen said with a little bow to Mrs. Maitland. "Thank you both."

Eastwood Manor wasn't overly large by aristocratic standards, and he found Miss Maitland with little trouble. She was seemingly lost in thought, admiring a stone statue that appeared to be of a roe deer as the wind tousled the curly brown hair that had managed to escape her bonnet, and Stephen cleared his throat.

"Oh, Mr. Eddington," she said, turning quickly toward him. "What a lovely surprise."

He tried desperately not to react, but he couldn't help the grin that spread across his face. He was a lovely surprise, was he?

"I am here mostly on behalf of my sister," he said, handing her the note Caroline had written. "She would like you to reconsider your attendance at her house party."

Miss Maitland accepted the note and took several moments to read it over. Then her hazel eyes met his. "Do you know what this says?"

Stephen shook his head, shifting his weight from one foot to the other. "Caroline didn't tell me exactly, only that she was disappointed you declined her invitation."

"She talks about how I can't ruin her reputation, how she's the daughter of a master builder married to the fifth son of an inconsequential gentleman, and no one in society even knows she exists," Miss Maitland explained.

"That is all true," Stephen replied, clasping his hands behind his back just to get them out of his way. "One or two society folks may know she exists, as they are aware I have a sister. But she has no dealings with them."

"I see." Miss Maitland's gaze traveled back to the note as a stiff breeze blew through, and she grasped firmly with both hands. "She also says that she would very much appreciate my company and that of my son."

Stephen nodded, even though she wasn't looking at him. "Caroline has been looking forward to having another woman of a similar age to talk to. And Patrick has been making lists of all the things he wants to show your son while they are here together."

Miss Maitland met his eyes again with a small smile. "Alex may go, of course, and stay until you tire of him."

"And you?" Her mouth turned down and Stephen quickly added, "If you don't feel comfortable staying at my home, you're welcome to come for as many or as few activities as you'd like, or to not come at all. The decision is yours to make."

She pressed her lips together as her eyes searched his face. Even the birds seemed to hold their collective breath, quietly waiting for her answer.

After a long moment, she exhaled slowly. "Might I have a day to think it over?"

"Yes, of course. But don't place more importance on this party than it warrants." He resisted the urge to reach out and touch her, though for some reason it took considerable willpower. "The point of this house party is for our two families to enjoy each others' company for a while, to enjoy having Patrick and Alex with us, and that's all. If that sounds like a pleasant way to spend your time, come. If it doesn't, we will see each other another time."

He was mentally berating himself for adding the last part—perhaps she didn't care if she saw him again—when she smiled faintly. It could have been his imagination, for it was gone as quickly as it appeared, but Stephen didn't think so.

"All right," she said, her voice maddeningly neutral. "I will be here tomorrow helping Adeleine and Natalie prepare for Natalie's next outing. If our paths don't cross, I'll send a note with a footman to your home."

They said their goodbyes and Stephen made his way back to the Maitland stables for his horse. Would she attend? Would she stay in his home?

Stephen couldn't come up with a believable reason to visit Philip Maitland again the next day, so he remained at home, catching up with his sister, playing games with his nieces and nephews, trying not to listen for a knock at the door.

When a footman in Maitland livery did finally arrive, Stephen's stomach did a little flip as he accepted the note with his name printed neatly upon it.

Dear Mr. Eddington,

On behalf of my son and myself, I thank you and your sister for the invitation to your house party. We are both pleased to attend for the duration. If your sister needs any help making arrangements, I am happy to assist her.

Margaret Maitland

"Caroline! She's coming!"

Caroline was at the front door with him a few moments later, clapping her hands together. "Wonderful! I'm so glad she changed her mind."

"I am too," he answered, scanning the note again.

He wasn't quite sure when it had happened, but sometime in the recent past Stephen had resolved to get to know Miss Maitland better. He was her brother's friend, after all, and they met often at Eastwood Manor.

Perhaps this house party was their chance to develop a relationship independent of their mutual connection.

Chapter 2

On THE APPOINTED DAY, MARGARET arrived at Mr. Eddington's home with her son, brother, and niece. Adeleine was feeling unwell, and decided to remain at home to rest. The carriage pulled smoothly up the circular drive and Margaret took the opportunity to stare before she put on her polite company demeanor. It was a modest house for a gentleman—two stories of gleaming red brick, an attic with a gray slate roof, and a few well-placed brick embellishments. Smaller in size than her brother's home, but with an air of understated charm.

The carriage came to a stop in front of the large, white front door just as a man and woman came out of the house and down the stone steps. The man was Mr. Eddington, dressed in a perfectly tailored forest green tailcoat, buff breeches, and shiny black top boots. The woman, who bore a marked resemblance to Mr. Eddington from the sandy brown hair and tall frame right down to the slightly crooked smile, wore a pink day dress with white lace flounces around the bottom.

They both stood back while one footman began gathering Margaret and Alex's baggage from the back of the carriage, and another let down the carriage steps and opened the door. Philip climbed out after Alex and offered his hand to his daughter, then to Margaret as they exited the carriage.

"Welcome," Mr. Eddington said when everyone had their feet firmly on the ground. He shook hands with Philip and Alex, and bowed swiftly to Margaret and Natalie. "Allow me to present my sister, Mrs. Gates. Caroline, this is Mr. Maitland…"

She offered her hand to Philip, who bowed over it politely. "A pleasure, madam."

"…Miss Maitland…"

Mrs. Gates smiled brightly at Margaret. "I'm so pleased you could join us."

Margaret found her enthusiasm charming and couldn't help but smile back. "So am I. It's lovely to meet you."

Alex and Natalie were both presented as well, then Mr. Eddington told them that Mrs. Gates's children were preparing to go fishing and where to find them. With silent assent from their respective parents, Alex and Natalie headed off to go find their companions. The two footmen gathered up the baggage and began carrying things into the house, and Philip and Mr. Eddington, already deep in conversation, followed slowly behind. That left Mrs. Gates and Margaret alone beside the carriage.

"How do you feel about gardens?" Mrs. Gates asked in a cheery voice. "There are four here, and each one has things I've never seen before."

"Wonderful," Margaret grinned. "My brother likes to call me the family's non-farming plant enthusiast, so I would love to see them."

The sun shone warmly overhead, and Mrs. Gates shaded her eyes. "Would you like to rest and refresh yourself first?"

Margaret shook her head. "It was just a short ride. Since the weather is fine, shall we spend some time in one of the gardens?"

Mrs. Gates linked her arm with Margaret's and led her around the side of the house. "This is a bit forward, as we've only just met, but I do hope you'll call me Caroline. With as much as my son and brother talk about you, I feel like I know you already."

Her son *and* her brother? Margaret expected the eldest Gates lad to know a bit about her, of course, as her own son's closest friend. But Mr. Eddington talked about her too?

Interesting.

Margaret ignored the little flutter in her stomach and focused on Caroline. "Then you must call me Margaret," she replied, trying to contain her excitement. Most of Margaret's friends had abandoned her twenty years ago when the rumor of her pregnancy was confirmed to be true. The few that maintained contact had gradually drifted away as their lives became very different from hers.

Perhaps this could be the start of something good, then.

Caroline practically hugged Margaret's arm. "Splendid! There is also something I would appreciate your help with, if you please."

"And what's that?"

Caroline loosened her hold a bit as the pair began to head toward the closest of the gardens. "My brother has held this property for nearly a year now, yet it has no name."

"Oh?"

"The previous owner never bothered to name it, and Stephen is more interested in how things run." Caroline swept her arm wide indicating the land around them. "I'm hoping that as we get to know this place, you and I can come up with a fitting name for it."

That was not something Margaret had ever been asked to do before, and she didn't quite know how to feel about the task. Naming a home was a rather intimate affair and, while she'd known Mr. Eddington for about a year now, they had never shared more than spirited conversation. But Caroline's bright eyes and wide smile suggested she was looking forward to tackling this challenge with her new friend.

"I bet we can," Margaret replied, her eyes sweeping over the verdant landscape. "Let's begin our investigation, shall we?"

Though it wasn't overly large, they spent the next few hours slowly exploring the garden closest to the house with its manicured lawn, its perfectly sculpted shrubbery, its stately old roses, talking and laughing as they shared stories and became better acquainted. They were still there when their flock of children returned with a respectable string of pungent fish carried proudly by the youngest Gates, who was quick to tell his mother all about how he'd been the most prolific of the bunch.

Caroline shot a look at Margaret that said, "back to reality" and took her youngest two by the hands, trying to listen to everyone talk at once. Alex sidled up beside her in Caroline's place, grinning.

"Did you have a nice time today?" she asked her son, tilting her head back slightly to meet his eyes. He looked more and more like his father every day, and Margaret felt a pang in her heart for what could have been.

"I did," he answered, offering his arm like a proper gentleman. "It was nice to be part of a big family for a while."

A thought popped out of Margaret's mouth before she could rein it in. "Did you ever wish you had siblings, Alex?"

She heard the wistfulness in her own voice and was not surprised when he took her hand and squeezed it. "Sometimes I did wonder what it would be like to have brothers and sisters. But then whenever I spend time with large families, like today, I'm very thankful that I was able to find peace and quiet, and time to myself when I needed it."

Margaret managed to partially suppress a smile and took her son's arm as they turned toward the house. "That was a very diplomatic answer."

"I know," he chuckled. Then he became a bit more serious. "But it was also the truth."

"You're a good lad."

He stopped walking and turned to her, studying her face. "Is all well with you, Mama? You haven't seemed like yourself since I arrived home."

"I haven't?" She was genuinely surprised to hear his assessment of her. She'd certainly been a bit deep in her memories lately like a man in his cups, but she hadn't thought anyone had noticed.

"No, you seem... You're quieter than usual, more contemplative."

She brushed a hand across his cheek. "I've missed you, that's all. Then you come home the very image of your father at that age..." She let her voice trail off, not knowing how to explain the painful happiness of a lost love to a young man who had not yet experienced it for himself. "I have been thinking about how different things could have been, but it's time to put that behind me now. We have plenty to look forward to."

"Including fish for supper," he said with a wink and steered them toward the house once more. "Patrick said that we're to have strawberries and cream for dessert, too."

Margaret grinned up at her son. "Now that is something to look forward to!"

Alex and Patrick, who were adults in truth and certainly old enough to eat in the dining room, had elected to spend the rest of the evening with the younger ones eating their catch, so Stephen and Philip met the ladies in the drawing room for a few minutes before going in to dinner rather informally. Stephen ended up sitting beside Miss Maitland, and the looks she shared with his sister across the table warmed his heart. Caroline didn't have many friends outside her own family, but it looked as though she may have a new one before this house party was over.

"You two clearly enjoyed your afternoon together," he remarked, glancing from Caroline to Miss Maitland.

Miss Maitland grinned. "We did." She took a bite of roasted potato and chewed thoughtfully. "It was wonderful to talk with someone who had some of the same experiences I've had. And the formal garden nearest the house is beautiful. What have you and my brother been up to?"

"The usual," Stephen said with an answering smile. "We mostly talked about farming techniques we might or might not try next year. Absolutely stimulating."

She put a hand to her mouth, but he noticed her giggle before she covered it.

"Adeleine has said that Philip speaks much less of farming to her since you took up residence here," Miss Maitland explained, "and for that you should receive a knighthood. The only two things Philip loves as much as his family are farming and politics."

"His love of farming has been extremely helpful to me," Stephen replied sincerely. "I learned how to construct a sturdy wall when I was a lad, but making things grow is not something I understood well. Your brother and my steward have taught me a tremendous amount in the past year."

"Philip is a good man to have around when you need support," she said softly, glancing across the table at her brother before spearing another piece of potato.

Stephen stared at his plate for a moment, continuing to cut and eat his food without tasting it, not knowing what to say. He knew that Philip Maitland had been instrumental in Alex's upbringing, but was unsure how to respond to such a serious statement from a woman he wasn't overly close to.

She saved him from the awkwardness a moment later. "I'm sorry, Mr. Eddington. That was perhaps more sentiment than is called for over dinner with one's neighbor."

"Not at all," he said, releasing a breath. "It's never wrong to heap praise upon someone who deserves it."

Her expression relaxed, as did her fingers which held her fork, and they spoke of more mundane things for a while. But there was one thing he had been wanting to ask her for some time now, and dinner in his own home seemed like the perfect opportunity.

"Will you call me Stephen? At least while you are here?"

She chewed slowly before answering. "Yes," she said with confidence. "If you will call me Margaret."

He bowed slightly from his chair. "It would be my pleasure, Margaret."

She offered him a stately nod. "And mine, Stephen."

The usual small talk permeated the rest of the meal, with the exception of Caroline telling the story about how Stephen's absolute best friend when he was nine years old had been a red squirrel that lived in a tree near their home, and at the conclusion of the last course the ladies elected to have their after dinner conversation in the drawing room.

"I know you will be departing soon," Stephen said to Philip, rising from the table, "but I have an excellent port if you'd like a glass."

"A fine idea," Philip replied, stretching as he stood. "That will give Natalie a bit more time with your nieces and nephews."

They settled in Stephen's library with their glasses of the sweet liquid, Stephen in the old green chair with fraying upholstery and Philip on the sofa near one of the tall windows. The fire that had burned in the grate that morning had been allowed to go out as the temperature rose outside, and a slight smokiness permeated the room.

"I'm going to ask you an impertinent question now that the women are out of hearing," Philip said as he looked around the room. "Why have you never married?"

That caught Stephen off guard. "What? Why?"

"You mentioned this afternoon wanting to be included in the more exclusive circles of society, and not for the first time." Philip added. "One way to do that is to marry into one. I was just thinking that it might be time for you to consider such a course of action."

"Oh, of course." Stephen consciously took a breath in and let it out. "For a moment I thought you had turned into my mother, insisting that it's time I found a wife and gave her grandchildren."

Philip's eyes went round. "Not me. I was lucky enough to meet Adeleine when we were young, and we've had so many happy years together. But I would never tell a grown man what to do with his life. It was merely a suggestion."

"A tried and true one, at that," Stephen replied, his voice and body relaxing into comfort once again. This was a thought he'd had many times himself. "A woman takes her social status from her husband, of course, but a wife's well-placed family members could introduce a man to the right people."

"That's it exactly," Philip said, gesturing with his glass. "You've done an admirable job of improving your circumstances, but if you want to be involved in government and politics, you need to know the right people and know them well. Adeleine's family was an enormous help when I stood for election."

Stephen laughed into his port. "Yes, because you, the cousin of a *duke*, were so very unknown."

Philip chuckled, too. "Third cousin," he clarified. "But yes, my own family name certainly opened some doors. It didn't hurt that I'm on good terms with my titled relations, either. You don't have that arrow in your quiver, though."

No, he didn't. The Eddington name didn't exactly carry a lot of weight in the circles Stephen hoped to one day travel in. If anything, it was a hindrance. "But a wife from the right family could mitigate my own genealogical shortcomings."

"You'll never work for the Prime Minister," Philip said, leaning against the back of the sofa. "You're over forty years of age. In addition to your parentage, you're far too old to be starting out in government—you'll be competing against younger men who have better connections. But you could eventually be appointed to a position that carries a great deal of influence."

Stephen was silent, soaking in those words. Could he reach so high? Even with the help of a wife from a "good" family, it would be difficult. It would be nigh on impossible with anyone else.

"I believe I could live with that," Stephen finally said, taking a large swallow of port. The change he could affect in such a position! Not nearly that of Philip's cousin, naturally, but far more than any Eddington had managed before him.

How much good could he do in the world with a position like that?

They talked abstractly about different positions that might suit Stephen, different families with eligible ladies, before Philip took his leave with promises to return the following day for the next slate of activities. But Stephen couldn't think about the house party, or anything else, for the rest of the evening. Philip Maitland thought he could rise to a high government position, if only he could find the right woman to wed.

His heart thudded as he recalled Margaret debating him over various things during dinner at Eastwood House, taking his arm as they walked toward the gate as they departed. His whole body warmed as he remembered all the times she'd touched him, leaned in closer to share an inside joke with him.

Then Stephen sighed deeply. Margaret, with her reputation, was certainly not the right woman to help him navigate the Beau Monde.

Chapter 3

"WE'RE PRACTICING ARCHERY THIS MORNING, Aunt Margaret," Natalie exclaimed when she and her father arrived the next day.

Margaret was seated at an escritoire in Stephen's morning room writing a letter as sunshine streamed in through the nearby window. She set her pen on the blotter to greet her niece. "Yes, and the butts are to be set up in Mr. Eddington's garden of exotic and unusual plants."

"Well, that will be interesting for you," Natalie replied brightly. "If you get tired of shooting arrows, you can study the plants.

Margaret smothered a chuckle as they headed out to the designated site. She was intrigued by a garden full of unusual plants and could undoubtedly spend many days examining them.

As they walked out, she trailed along behind the crowd, taking in the absolute beauty of the place. The sun was shining in a brilliant blue sky, casting its warm rays over the lush green grass and the multitude of plants that she'd never seen outside of botany texts.

"Did you sleep well last night?" Caroline asked, coming up beside her.

"Like I didn't have a care in the world," Margaret answered with a contented sigh. "I can't remember the last time I was that comfortable, even in my own bed."

"Excellent," Caroline replied, linking her arm with Margaret's as they walked. "Perhaps you'd enjoy a bit of competition, then?"

Margaret turned to look at her companion. "Competition? You mean at archery?"

Caroline nodded and Stephen's voice piped up from behind them, "It's not too late, Philip—your sister hasn't agreed to anything yet."

"What am I about to agree to?" Margaret asked him, noting her brother on Stephen's other side.

Stephen drew even with the two women and slowed to keep pace with them. "Caroline is about to suggest that the two of you could easily shoot better than the two of us, and that we could make things interesting with a little wager."

Caroline grinned. "I wasn't going to suggest a wager, but that is a fine idea."

"I suppose you weren't going to suggest an amount, either?" Stephen asked warily.

Philip shook his head. "Not money. I want to win the ability to do something..."

"Or to make someone else do something," Margaret finished with a grateful glace at her brother. She had some money of her own, but did not possess the fortunes that the other three did.

"I haven't scheduled any activities for Saturday yet," Caroline said, meeting Margaret's eyes and winking.

"Perhaps the winning team could choose how we spend our time that day, then," Margaret finished for her.

Philip rolled his eyes but they were twinkling when he spoke. "You were wrong, Eddington—it *is* too late."

Stephen's gaze shifted from his sister to Margaret and lingered there for a moment before he answered. "I don't see any way around it, then. We're going to have to accept the challenge."

"And be gracious in our victory, of course," Philip said with a chuckle.

"Your victory," Margaret snorted. "We'll just see, won't we?"

When they arrived at the archery butts the servants had set up, the children were already selecting bows and arrows, and arguing over who was going to shoot at which target. The adults took up their equipment and paired off, with Caroline and Margaret choosing the last target in the line and Stephen and Philip setting up next to them.

"Five practice shots, then we start," Caroline announced. Then, quietly, she said to Margaret, "You have done this before, haven't you?"

"Oh yes," Margaret answered with relish. "Philip and I took lessons with the same archery master when we were children. Much to his chagrin, I was as good as he was, though I am three years younger."

"Wait," Stephen called, holding both his hands out in a "stop" gesture. "How are we going to hold each team accountable?"

Philip's mouth turned down in a hard frown. "Is not our honor good enough?"

Caroline made a little waving motion with one hand. "It's me he's worried about, Mr. Maitland, not you or Margaret. Once, when I was very young, I miscounted the number of points I'd scored in some game, and Stephen has brought it up each and every time we are involved in something competitive."

Philip still looked unsettled at the idea of labeling a lady as a cheat, but Margaret had a very sensible way to resolve the problem. "All right then, why don't Mr. Eddington and I use this target? Philip, you and Caroline can use that one. The sexes are separated, as are the sibling pairs."

Stephen's eyes fixed on hers and they shared a... A moment? A thought?

A wish?

Whatever it was, the connection was broken when he looked away to gather up his bow and arrows. "Yes, I think that will do nicely."

Caroline and Stephen switched positions, and Margaret's heart fluttered as he came toward her. But she gave herself a mental shake and tried to relax her body. It was just a game, and she was merely shooting a bow at the same target as her neighbor, her brother's friend. Nothing more.

Unless...

"Thank you for sharing some of your good sense with us, Margaret," Stephen said in a voice only loud enough for her to hear. "Caroline and I are close in age, and did many things together as children."

Margaret offered him a knowing smile. "So you have a long history of watching each other carefully so there are no unfair advantages. Philip and I have a similar relationship."

"I would trust my sister with my very life," Stephen told her, taking a step closer.

"But not with the scoring of a game," Margaret added, the corners of her mouth turning up slightly. "Yes, Philip and I are much the same, and so is my son with his cousins."

Stephen chuckled, leaning on his bow as if it were a walking stick. "A common sentiment among family members, then. I just didn't want you to think…"

His voice trailed off and it was Margaret's turn to step closer. "That you were some kind of scoundrel with no honor? No," she shook her head, as the gentle breeze tousled the loose strands of her hair. "If that were the case, neither Philip nor Adeleine would have ever invited you into their home, let alone ask you to return… How many times?"

"Scores," he replied, the corners of his eyes crinkling up with his smile.

"Well, there you are. My brother and his wife are good, proper people," she said, laying her fingers on his arm for the briefest of touches. "Though they make an exception for me, of course."

Why did she say that? If she could have taken those last words back, she would have immediately. Margaret thought she'd done away with the self-deprecating jokes years ago, as they tended to draw more attention to her situation rather than lighten the mood.

But apparently not.

"That is where you're wrong—you need no exception," Stephen told her quietly. He dropped his eyes to fish around in the pile for an arrow he liked, then met her gaze again, though the intensity and solemnity they had just shared blew away in the light wind. "Shall we?" He asked, gesturing with his arrow toward their target.

"Yes," she answered smoothly, "I think we'd better before we fall behind."

She watched as Stephen took his practice shots, meticulous about his aim and grip on both the bow and arrow, not letting the arrow fly until he was sure everything was satisfactory. Had he been as deliberate when he said she needed no exception to be included in her brother's proper household?

Did he believe her to be a respectable lady despite her past?

Margaret shoved that thought right out of her mind. She was here to seek out the possibility of new friendships, full stop. There was no point in following any other path when it would only lead to humiliation and heartbreak.

After dinner that evening, Stephen and Philip elected not to go off on their own, but joined the ladies in the drawing room.

"No Natalie tonight?" Stephen asked as he took a seat beside Margaret on a hard sofa. He needed to have a word with his housekeeper, or possibly his sister, about replacing the awful thing with something worth sitting on.

"She had a marvelous time this afternoon," Philip answered from his chair opposite the sofa, "but her mother needed her at home this evening."

Margaret sipped her sherry. "I believe they were studying rules of etiquette."

Stephen groaned. "That brings back some memories I'd rather forget."

"For me, too," Margaret said with a chuckle. "Adeleine tries to explain the circumstances rules are meant for, which seems to help Natalie."

"What helps Natalie?" a young man asked.

The joy that overcame Margaret at the sight of her son was palpable. Alex followed Caroline and her eldest son into the room, and Margaret was positively luminous. "Alex! And

Patrick! I thought you were spending time with the younger ones."

Alex settled himself on a settee that creaked slightly under his weight. "We decided our time would be better spent with adults this evening."

Caroline sat in the chair beside Philip and practically cackled. "Tired, are you?"

Patrick forwent the creaky settee and brought another chair over from near the fireplace. He sat down in it with a sigh. "Yes. Uncle Stephen, if you ever have children of your own, make sure you have plenty of people to help you take care of them."

"Fortunately, you have your mother, father, a governess, and a nurse to help you take care of your brothers and sisters," Stephen quipped, picking up his glass of port. He didn't take a drink, but he felt as if he needed to do something with his hands.

Alex, thankfully, jumped in and changed the subject. "So who won your archery wager?"

"Oh yes! And what are we doing on Saturday?" Patrick chimed in.

"Believe it or not, it was a draw," Margaret answered, resting her sherry glass carefully on her knee. "So we have to come up with something that all four of us would enjoy."

The conversation turned to different activities they could do in an afternoon from riding to painting to just having an afternoon with nothing planned, and Stephen found his mind wandering. He didn't much care what was planned or not planned, he was simply enjoying spending time with his family and friends.

And perhaps taking advantage of their knowledge.

"Margaret, might I ask a favor of you?" he said, leaning slightly toward her as the others continued to talk around them.

"Certainly," she replied. "How can I be of service?"

Was it his imagination or was that the faintest hint of perfume he detected? He didn't recall her wearing any fragrances for dinners with her brother. "The garden we were in this afternoon is where the previous owner placed exotic specimens and interesting plants that could thrive in our climate."

"Oh yes," Margaret said, her eyes bright. "I noticed some stunning hydrangeas by the statue of Atalanta."

There was only one statue in that garden, and Stephen pictured the white flowers that clumped almost in spheres that evoked the feeling of snowballs even as the sun shone warmly overhead. "Is that what those are?"

She grinned. "Yes. Is that what you need help with? Identifying plants?"

"It is," he said, taking a drink of his port. "Caroline mentioned that you were the Maitland interested in non-farming plants, and I was hoping that while you were here..."

"I would love to," she said when his voice trailed off.

"Marvelous," he said, relief flooding through him. "Neither my head gardener nor his assistant know what most of the plants are in that garden, nor how to take care of them. The previous owner apparently handled that area himself, and would sometimes issue orders but never explained anything to them."

Margaret glanced at the others in the room and must have been satisfied by what she saw, for her shoulders relaxed when she turned back to him. "I have some botany texts at home that may be of help. Perhaps we can walk over one day this week and collect them."

"I appreciate whatever knowledge you have to share," he told her, stifling the urge to punctuate his point by taking her hand. He'd never done such a thing before, nor had it ever occurred to him, but for some reason he very much wanted to now.

"How does that sound to you?" Caroline asked, breaking his thoughts and bringing him back to the larger conversation.

"How does what sound?" he asked cheerfully.

Caroline lifted one eyebrow briefly, but continued on serenely, "Mr. Maitland and I thought an afternoon in the village would be a good way to spend Saturday."

"We can do some shopping, purchase some treats," Philip added. "And I heard that the blacksmith has a litter of puppies who will be weaned soon."

Patrick grinned at the mention of puppies and Stephen winked at his sister. "We'll definitely have to see the puppies."

"I think it's a splendid idea," Margaret said, and Stephen saw her shoot him a look he couldn't quite identify. "Shall we take the little ones or do you think they'd be better off here with their nurse?"

"Do we have enough conveyances for everyone?" Stephen asked. An adult could walk into the village from his home, but it was a long walk and the smaller children wouldn't be able to manage it.

The six of them discussed details, but Stephen was only partially participating in the conversation. With Margaret's enthusiastic agreement to help him identify the unknown plants in his garden—and also because this was an excellent opportunity to do something nice for her in general—he was trying to decide how to repay the favor. His first thought was manual labor, but she lived in the dower house on her brother's estate and Philip had mentioned once or twice that she had her own small staff. Stephen didn't know her exact financial situation, but he gathered that she didn't need help there either.

Perhaps he could find a gift for her when they made their trip into the village in a few days. Did she work outside in her own garden? Was she fond of pastries? Would she appreciate a book or a handkerchief or puppy?

He stopped himself from physically shaking his head since he was surrounded by people, but he was stumped. Margaret Maitland was not one to tell all to anyone except those who were closest to her, and perhaps not even them. He would simply have to pay more attention to the thoughts and feelings she did express.

Chapter 4

I T TOOK THREE CARRIAGES TO transport them all to the village, and they must have looked like a swarming horde of locusts descending upon the blacksmith's forge: Stephen, Philip and Adeleine with Natalie, Caroline and her five children, Alex, and finally Margaret, who allowed her son to help her down then discreetly stretched her legs and back. The distance from Stephen's home to the village was only a few miles, but the older she grew the less comfortable traveling any distance became.

The younger children were given strict instructions to remain with at least one person over the age of sixteen at all times, then the horde dispersed and the carriage drivers guided their vehicles away. Margaret stood alone and looked about her in mild disbelief. One would never know that the people of three separate households had overrun the place just moments ago.

But all was quiet now and she breathed deeply, filling her lungs to capacity before slowly exhaling. The smell of horses and metal permeated the air when she faced the forge, but she could detect baking bread and grass when she turned toward the village center. Children were playing in the distance, artfully dodging adults to retrieve their ball when it rolled away into the dirt road.

Where should she go? She'd been pondering that question since they'd agreed to make this trip, yet was still unsure. Some shops she knew to stay away from—the dressmaker who wouldn't allow her to even walk through the door, the tea shop where they would happily take her money but snicker and whisper behind her back, the milliner who apologized profusely while explaining that Margaret's presence would drive away too many of her customers.

It all felt petty and mean-spirited after all these years, but Margaret didn't waste energy fighting their decisions now, as she hadn't when her son was born. She was extremely fortunate in the support of her family, both emotional and financial, and simply took her business elsewhere.

Like to the baker who made the most divine shortbread this side of Hadrian's Wall.

"Miss Maitland!" he exclaimed when she entered the shop. "What a pleasant surprise! Oh, and you're just in time—I took a batch of shortbread out of the oven just moments ago."

Margaret couldn't help but rub her hands together with anticipation. She could practically taste the buttery confection just from the smell of the bakery alone. "Mr. Ralston, it's lovely to see you again. How is Mrs. Ralston?"

"She's very well, thank you for asking," he replied, his smile becoming tight. "She asked me to thank you for sending over all those newspapers. They have been her main form of entertainment for the past fortnight, and she's very grateful to have them."

Hmm. If Mrs. Ralston was spending all her time reading rather than her usual knitting, her arthritis must be paining her more than usual.

Margaret made a mental note to send her maid over to the Ralstons to help with the household work and whatever else they might need.

She stayed for several minutes to talk with Mr. Ralston a bit more, and to purchase her weight in shortbread, then said her goodbyes and decided to visit the bookshop down the way. Between the financial support of her brother and her cousin Cecilia, Margaret's needs were more than met and she had enough pin money to purchase a few luxuries each month. Books were normally not among them, as she had Philip's entire library to choose from, but her choice of reading material didn't always align with his.

She entered the shop quietly, nodding to a patron in a plain yellow dress who passed her. Margaret saw the woman's eyes widen and watched her immediately rush to another part of the room.

Blast.

Would she draw attention to herself if she turned right around and left the shop? Or should she casually circumnavigate the shelves then slip out? Margaret didn't recognize the woman who'd walked past her, but she'd seen that expression too many times before.

"Miss Maitland?"

Margaret turned to find the owner of the shop standing just in front of the woman in yellow. *Too late.*

"Miss Margaret Maitland?"

"Yes, I am Margaret Maitland." There was an edge to her voice that she attempted to soften, but was not entirely successful in doing so.

The owner cleared his throat. "Then I'm afraid I'm going to have to ask you to leave."

Margaret's jaw clenched. "For what reason? I've only just come in. I haven't even had a chance to look at anything yet."

"You know the reason," the owner answered, lowering his voice.

The woman in yellow crossed her arms and cocked one eyebrow as if to challenge Margaret, to goad her into some inappropriate reaction. But Margaret only rolled her eyes. She opened her mouth to speak but was startled to hear a familiar voice only steps behind her.

"Did you just tell this lady to leave?" Stephen asked, coming to a halt beside her. He was tall and broad and glowering at the shop owner.

Margaret's heartbeat thudded in her ears and all she could do was stare dumbly at her neighbor.

"I did," the shop owner said, dropping the volume of his voice another notch. "This is a respectable business, and people like her are not welcome here."

"Is that what *you* think, or what this one told you to think?" Stephen asked gruffly, nodding in the direction of the woman in yellow. "Is there nothing in your past that people might judge you for if they knew about it?"

The shop owner had the grace to blush and look down at his feet for the briefest of moments, but when the woman in yellow poked his shoulder, he shook his head. "My choices are not at issue. Miss Maitland is not welcome here."

Margaret furtively reached over and touched a finger to Stephen's arm, silently willing him to give up the argument and escort her out of the shop. There was nothing either of them could say that would change the owner's mind, and Margaret did not want to spend another moment in a place where she was treated this way.

"That's fine," Stephen replied, his voice as smooth as the Irish whiskey in Philip's study. "No one from my household will shop here again, and I expect Philip Maitland will feel the same way."

He offered his arm to Margaret, who took it with relief and strode out, unable to resist a look back at the dismayed shop owner and the frowning woman in yellow.

When they were far away from the shop, Margaret stopped walking but held Stephen's arm. "You didn't have to do that."

He turned to face her, briefly covering her hand with his. "I have no doubt that you could have handled that situation perfectly well on your own. I'm sure you've done it before, more times than you can count. But fighting the same battle over and over can be tiring, and I thought I might provide some assistance."

She met his eyes, noting that they were several shades lighter than the blue of the sky above them, and gave his arm a slight squeeze.

"I always appreciate reinforcements," she said softly.

"I am available any time you might need me," he replied with a small smile.

They resumed walking, their pace relaxed, the distance between them—physical and emotional—shrinking with every step.

Stephen rode home in his own carriage with Margaret and three of Caroline's children, instructing the driver to detour to the dower house at Eastwood Manor before returning to his own front door. The stop at Margaret's home was a short one—just long enough for her to go in and collect some of her books while he entertained the children. He would have much preferred to walk over with her, as she'd previously suggested, without the company of his nieces and nephews, but this way they avoided the appearance of improper behavior. After the incident in the bookshop he needed to take better care with her reputation, despite her insistence that her reputation was ruined long ago. There was no need to throw any more fuel on a fire that was still smoldering.

Not that the children were fit chaperones, of course, and no one would take their word for anything if someone started an unsavory rumor. But he felt better having someone with them who was old enough to speak about what they saw and heard.

It wasn't until after dinner that he was able to talk to Margaret in a more private setting, though "private" was a relative term. The ladies and gentlemen gathered in the drawing room together again, and Stephen entered after most of the other guests, having a pleasant conversation with Mrs. Maitland as they strolled from the dining room. Margaret had managed to make a two seats in the corner of the drawing room both secluded and public at the same time—two wingback chairs had been pulled close beside one another facing the center of the room. She sat in one with a stack of books at her feet, and gestured him over.

Stephen excused himself to Mrs. Maitland and made his way over to the empty chair beside Margaret, his grin growing as he approached. They hadn't had a chance to discuss the books in much depth in the carriage with three very tired and out of sorts children, so he had been looking forward to this with great anticipation. "What a treasure trove of information you've brought."

"I have some botany books, and some that tend more toward horticulture," she said, setting the one she was reading on the arm of the chair within his view.

"What's the difference?"

"Botany is the study of plants," she explained, a slight wrinkle forming between her eyes as she considered her words. "Horticulture is more specifically the study of gardens."

He shifted in his seat a bit so he could comfortably read the pages of the book on the chair's arm. "Oh, I see. So horticulture is like a specialty within the larger field of botany."

"Yes, exactly." She flipped the pages of the book on the chair arm until she found the one she wanted. "And see here, this looks like one of the plants I saw in your mystery garden the other day."

He leaned forward to study the drawing of plant with long, wide leaves that formed a low mass with a flower spike rising above it, but was distracted by the delicate scent of her perfume. What was it? Had she chosen it specially for this evening?

He closed his eyes for the merest of moments to try to focus on the picture in the book. "It certainly is. There is a group of them in a shady area under a stand of trees."

"They are called hostas, originally grown in Japan and China."

She pointed to a section of text and he read for himself about *hosta ventricosa*, how it could grow up to three feet wide and could not tolerate much sun. "Amazing! Does it say how to take care of them?"

They leafed through her books, marking useful pages with bits of paper so Stephen could go back to them later. Later, when he was not trying to catalog the fragrance of her perfume with half his brain while the other half tingled at every accidental brush of her fingers as they turned pages.

"Can I ask you an impertinent question?" she asked softly as she opened another book on top of the one they were looking through.

She kept her eyes on the pages before them, her eyelashes concealing the sentiment behind her words, and it took every ounce of willpower he had to answer in a steady voice. "Ask away."

"Why did you get involved at the bookshop this afternoon?" She turned a page slowly. "You could have simply escorted me out to avoid causing a scene or ignored the whole affair entirely. But you didn't."

A sudden rush of anxiety filled his body as memories from his university days came flooding back, and he fought to relax. "I know how it feels to be seen as lesser, to be rejected simply for who you are."

"You do?"

"I am the son of a tradesman, remember?" He tightened every muscle in his body for a moment, then relaxed them. That helped, but didn't slow his pounding heart. "My father worked for a living, which made me an outcast before I even arrived some places. Cambridge especially."

Her hazel eyes slowly lifted to meet his. "Oh, goodness. Yes, Philip and Alex have both told me stories about the treatment of students who attended, but didn't come from the 'right' families."

"The Eddingtons are not one of the 'right' families," he replied, then paused to clear his throat. "It never mattered how much money we had nor how intelligent I was. My father worked for a living, and that meant I was unwelcome."

Her fingers brushed against his once more, but this time she didn't move them away. "And it all came back when the bookshop owner tried to throw me out."

"Yes," he croaked.

She was silent for a long moment, her face completely unreadable, and Stephen began to regret his disclosure. It was the truth, but he could have chalked his actions up to mere gallantry, coming to the defense of his friend's sister. Had this confession been too intimate?

"I was betrothed to Alex's father when I was twenty," she responded. Her voice was steady but her eyes had returned to the book's pages. "Both families were satisfied with the match and we were very much in love— everything was perfect."

"Until it wasn't."

She nodded, swallowing audibly. "One day he just disappeared. His family didn't know where he'd gone, his friends hadn't seen him, no one knew what happened to him. And we'd... anticipated our vows. It wasn't long before I suspected I was with child, and every month that passed confirmed it."

"He got you with child then left you?" Stephen's fingers began to curl into a fist.

"That's what everyone thought," Margaret continued, putting a hand on his sleeve as if to calm him. "It was a full year before he could even get a letter to his family—he'd been impressed."

"Impressed into the Royal Navy?" Stephen asked in disbelief. He knew what impressment was, but he'd never actually known anyone who had been taken.

She nodded weakly. "Forced to serve aboard a ship. By the time he returned to England, Alex was walking and talking." She took a deep breath and blew it out slowly. "Alex's father attempted to pick up where we left off, but the damage to my reputation was already done and he was... He was never the same after his ordeal."

Stephen pressed his lips together, determined that the next words out of his mouth would be supportive, but she beat him to it.

"I was lucky, though," she told him, her voice growing stronger. "I had Philip, my parents, my cousin Cecilia to support me. They were the reason I could even entertain the possibility of keeping my child. I could have ended my pregnancy. I could have hidden it, gone away to some distant relative to have the baby and give him away. I could have pretended the whole thing never happened and returned to my life."

"But you didn't." Most women in her position did end pregnancies or bear their children in secret. To raise an illegitimate child in the open was social death, and for most women of Margaret's class that meant a lifetime of isolation and struggle.

She shook her head and the scent of her perfume swirled through the air. "My family allowed me to make the decision myself and supported me when I did. I knew what I was giving up when I decided to raise my child, but I also knew that he'd never want for anything.

Most women in my position aren't so fortunate."

They sat together in a silence that gradually shifted from angry to sympathetic, her hand still on his sleeve, his head bent toward hers.

"I believe we have both been fortunate in our families," he finally said, his voice quiet but steady.

"Yes," she agreed, meeting his eyes once more. "We have."

Chapter 5

MARGARET SAT AT THE BREAKFAST table the next morning, picking at the plate of food before her. There were fresh fruits and vegetables from the kitchen garden, crispy toast to which she'd applied a generous coating of butter and strawberry jam, even eggs, which she hadn't had for breakfast in years. A steaming cup of strong tea sat beside her plate, the aroma tickling her mind and bringing back memories of Alex's father, who always drank his tea as strong as it could be brewed.

Her memories contrasted sharply with the scene playing out before her eyes, though. Alex and Patrick sat a little apart from her on one side of the table, with Stephen across from them. The three men were having a spirited discussion regarding Napoleon's recent surrender aboard the HMS *Bellerophon* to Captain Frederick Maitland, a rather distant cousin. Alex's eyes were bright, his hands gesturing as he spoke, as they always did when he was excited about the topic of discussion. Patrick, likewise, was leaning forward, his cheeks pink with the enthusiasm of his words.

But in this instance, it wasn't the younger men that had captured so much of Margaret's attention. It was Stephen. He was just as eager and lively as Alex and Patrick, debating and correcting but also listening carefully to what each one had to say. He was careful to look them in the eye when they were talking, to let them finish their thoughts before countering, nodding vigorously when he agreed. While some of Stephen and Margaret's generation were dismissive of younger adults, continually treating them as the children they no longer were, Stephen responded to Alex and Patrick as if they were his equals.

Margaret lifted her teacup to her lips and realized he interacted with everyone the same way—younger adults, servants, peers, his social superiors.

A lady who had borne an illegitimate child.

"What do you think, Mama?" Alex asked.

She smiled at him, her sweet boy all grown up. "I'm sorry, I was woolgathering. What do I think about what?"

"I ride the entire estate every few days so I can keep abreast of what is happening where. I would like to take Patrick and Alex out with me today, if you don't mind."

"I don't mind at all," Margaret replied, hoping she hid her surprise well enough. Did Stephen realize the symbolism this ride could have? Had she wed Alex's father as planned, *he* would be the one riding out with their son, looking over the property Alex would one day inherit. "I noticed stacks of clouds on the horizon when I was out for my walk this morning—hopefully you don't get caught in the rain."

The men stayed for a few minutes more before pushing their chairs back and bidding Margaret goodbye. She gave them a cheerful wave, meeting Stephen's blue eyes and holding his gaze for a moment. He offered her a small nod, smiled, then turned to follow the others.

She was sure of it now. He knew exactly what he'd asked, and how she would interpret it.

Her heart thudded in her ears and a little tingle ran down her spine. Stephen Eddington was courting her.

"Oh, goodness."

"What's wrong?"

Margaret started, setting her teacup down in its saucer with a clank. "Oh, Philip, I didn't see you there."

He moved from his place in the doorway and settled into the chair beside hers. "I only just arrived. I ran into Eddington on my way in —he's taking Alex and Patrick out to ride the estate?"

Margaret nodded slowly. "He is."

Philip's eyebrows rose. "I see. Well, I came to find you to see if you were all right after last evening, but things have clearly progressed beyond that."

"To see if I was all right?"

"Yes." He folded his hands and rested them on his knee. "You and Eddington seemed to be quite comfortable with your botany books yesterday after dinner. But by the end of the evening the two of you looked as though you'd been through something terrible together."

Margaret sighed deeply. "Both of your observations are true, I think." Philip's forehead wrinkled in confusion, and she continued, "We started off with the books and made good progress identifying some of the plants in his garden. But then..."

She described Stephen's actions in the bookshop, and Philips expression relaxed. "I'm sorry I wasn't there for you myself, but I'm glad he was."

"When we were looking through my books yesterday, I asked him why he'd helped me," she continued softly. "And it turns out that we have had some of the same experiences in our lives."

"Oh, of course. Yes, he's had a difficult time breaking into certain circles because of his parentage," Philip said. "And you have been on the outside looking in as well."

"Yes."

Philip mulled that information over for a moment. "And now he's taking Alex out to ride his estate."

Margaret nodded again. "Yes."

"Are you two...?"

His eyes dropped to the table, to her hand resting near the handle of her fragile teacup painted with delicate little flowers. "We haven't made each other any promises."

Philip leaned forward slightly. "Would you like to?"

"What I would like doesn't matter," Margaret made herself say aloud. Then she glanced up at her big brother. "Philip, I would be such a hindrance to him. He needs a wife he can take to social functions, not one who will be turned away at the door. Someone who will be the perfect hostess for political dinners, not one who is the butt of lewd jokes."

Philip cringed, no doubt remembering several of the instances in which he defended his sister's honor after Alex was born. Then he laid a finger on her chin and turned her head toward his. "But if none of that mattered, would you want to marry him?"

She hesitated. "Perhaps. I... I hadn't thought about it until yesterday." She stood, taking a step away from the table and her brother. "But you told me yourself that Stephen has plans to climb through the ranks of government, so my reputation does matter. It matters a great deal."

Philip rose from his chair and set his arm about her shoulders. "Have you spoken to him about this?"

"No," she said taking a deep breath and exhaling slowly. "I'm not entirely sure there's anything to discuss yet, and I don't want to be presumptuous."

"Given the way he's been looking at you—these past few days especially—I seriously doubt you'd be wrong," Philip replied.

"How does he look at me?"

Philip grinned. "Have you not noticed? He looks at you the same way I look at Adeleine."

Her brother worshiped his wife, and always had. Was that how Stephen felt about her? Margaret sighed again, trying to stem the tide of emotions that threatened to overwhelm her. "Oh."

"Oh indeed."

"Has he said anything to you?" she asked suddenly.

Philip shook his head. "It's not as though he needs my permission, or Father's for that matter. But you will be the first to know if he speaks to me about you."

"Stephen may not need your permission, but I might need your counsel," she said, leaning her head against his shoulder.

"You will have it," Philip promised. "Anytime you need it."

When Stephen returned to the house that afternoon, he managed to sneak away to his study where he could give his neglected correspondence his full attention. He knew he had at least two hours before he needed to dress for dinner, so he pulled the pile of letters into the center of his overlarge desk and started sorting them into piles according to their urgency. Some letters he'd previously read but had put aside to deal with later, and some hadn't even been opened yet. He took the time to at least skim all of them until one massive pile of stationary turned into three: things that must be dealt with now, things that could wait until after his guests returned to their homes, and things that he could hand off to his steward.

He was halfway through answering the letters that required immediate attention when a knock sounded on the stout door. "Enter," he called, continuing to write.

His butler or a footman would have entered and waited to be acknowledged, but the person who opened the door did not. "Are you busy?"

"Caroline." He glanced at his letter and decided it could wait a few more minutes. "I need a break anyway—my hand is starting to cramp."

She made her way across the room, her footsteps echoing on the bare wooden floor, and perched on the edge of the sofa. "I just wanted to check on you. You seemed upset after your talk with Margaret in the drawing room last night, but I didn't want to say anything in front of the children or her family."

He went to sit beside her, and blew out a breath as he lowered himself onto the sofa. "Oh, right. All is well. I interceded on her behalf at a shop when we were in the village the other day, and when we spoke about it last evening it stirred up some memories I'd rather like to forget. That's all."

"You interceded on her behalf?"

Caroline asked the question as if she already knew the details, so Stephen supplied a quick summary of the encounter in the bookshop. "I've been in that position before, been the one who was unwelcome because of who I was. I couldn't just let that happen to Margaret."

"Stephen, I'm going to ask you a delicate question, and I'd like you to answer me honestly."

"Of course I will," he responded, a note of annoyance in his voice.

"Are you in love with Margaret Maitland?"

She spoke the words quietly, as if she were trying to keep them within the confines of the sofa, and Stephen didn't fully comprehend them at once. "Am I... Am I in love with Margaret?"

Caroline nodded. "Yes, that is what I asked."

He slid back, relaxing his body against the back of the sofa. "I don't know."

"That's not a 'no' though," Caroline replied matter-of-factly, turning sideways to face him.

"No, it isn't." His gaze dropped to Caroline's shoulder as he thought about his interactions with Margaret, recently and over the year he'd known her. He certainly felt *something* for her that was different from the friendship he had with his other neighbors. She was kind, caring, generous to others regardless of their station in life. She had taken to Caroline as if they'd been lifelong friends despite the differences in their circumstances. And she understood him in ways not even his own sister did.

Caroline had led a fairly sheltered life. She was educated at home by a governess, socialized with the children of their parents' friends, met her husband through a mutual acquaintance. Thankfully, outside of one or two high sticklers, she had encountered very little opposition in her life.

But Margaret had, like him, been an outsider in her own social circle. They had both committed the sin of being different from the expectations others held for them. He'd had friends, particularly at Cambridge, who were also outsiders for one reason or another, but he could never talk about it with them the way he did with Margaret. Sharing with her the memories, the feelings he'd shoved deep down inside himself had just felt right.

Had Margaret felt it too?

Stephen forced his eyes to focus on his sister's face. "I don't think I'm in love with her yet."

"Yet?" Caroline fairly pounced on the word.

Stephen's answering smile started out small, but when he allowed himself to picture a future with Margaret by his side, it grew into a full fledged grin. "Yet."

"Does she know?"

He shook his head. "I don't think so. We haven't talked about it, at least."

Caroline clasped her hands in her lap, likely to keep herself still. "You'll dance with her at Miss Natalie's practice ball, though, won't you?"

Stephen had completely forgotten about that event, and it was happening in just a few days. "I will ask her for at least one dance yes."

"Wonderful." She rose from the sofa, grinning. "Good luck."

Caroline let herself out of the study, leaving Stephen alone with his thoughts in the rather somber room full of dark woods and heavy fabrics. He could almost feel Margaret's hands in his as they danced a country dance or a staid old quadrille. There was no way Mrs. Maitland would allow a waltz, but perhaps he and Margaret could find a quiet place to admire the stars.

Unless she rejected his advances, of course, for that was a distinct possibility. His heart sank at the mere thought of it, then sank even deeper into the gloom of heartache when he realized the possible consequences of his future actions. If he did end up wedding Margaret, what would happen to his career in government? Philip had said that Stephen could rise high if he had a respectable wife from the "right" kind of family. The Maitlands were certainly the "right" kind of family, but Margaret herself was looked down upon in society even more than he was. Would her past hinder his future?

Was he willing to risk it?

And what if Margaret was unwilling or uninterested in becoming his wife? His relationship with her brother would surely change, and not for the better. Would his sister's budding friendship with Margaret wither too?

Stephen dropped his head into his hands. Perhaps the best thing he could do for Caroline and himself was to just pretend that Margaret was simply the sister of his good friend and neighbor, to ignore the feelings that had been percolating through his body. Although, based on the ease with which he spilled out the most private parts of his life to her, pretending might not be enough. He may have to avoid Margaret altogether.

"I should have asked Mr. Mowbray's daughter for her hand last year and been done with it," Stephen said aloud, sliding his hands down his face and letting them fall into his lap. Louisa would have been the perfect wife for a person with ambitions of government service and politics, and she seemed genuinely interested in Stephen as a person.

But he never felt comfortable sharing the ups and downs of his life with Louisa Mowbray.

A muffled gong sounded from deeper within the house, signaling the dinner hour.

Well, there were three more days until Miss Natalie's practice ball. He had until then to figure out who, or what, was most important to him.

Chapter 6

MARGARET WALKED OVER TO EASTWOOD Manor after luncheon with the gown she planned to wear at Natalie's practice ball draped over one arm. The pasture was still damp with dew and she stepped carefully through the grass—this was the favorite grazing site of Eastwood's dairy cows—glad Caroline's lady's maid had thought to wrap her evening gown in an old bedsheet.

She'd promised her niece she would come over early to assist with preparations, but when she arrived Adeleine had everything well in hand.

"Is there anything at all I can help with?" Margaret asked, watching footmen roll up the carpets in the music room and carefully remove most of the furniture.

Adeleine pooched her lips out for a moment, as she often did when she thinking. "This," she said, gesturing around the room, "is all going as planned. But perhaps you could sit with Natalie for a while? I did for a bit this morning, but she's nervous and doesn't want her mother hovering."

"Of course. Where is she?" Margaret asked, relieved. She was ready to pitch in wherever she was needed, but her head was elsewhere and she wasn't sure she could be trusted with details just now.

"She's planted herself in the morning room —away from the commotion, she said."

Margaret chuckled. "So much like her father sometimes. You should have seen Philip before his first ball."

Adeleine laughed. "I remember him hiding in the card room for at least half of it," she said. "He does like to socialize with friends, with people he knows well, but not with strangers."

"I'll remind Natalie that there are no strangers coming tonight," Margaret replied, moving toward the door. "Perhaps that will ease her mind."

Margaret found her niece in the morning room as stated, staring at a blank piece of paper with pen poised. "Are you writing letters? If I'm disturbing you, I can come back."

Natalie set her pen down and sighed. "I thought perhaps writing letters would help to pass the time, but I can't seem to find the words for anything."

"Are the words not coming to you, or are you unable to focus long enough to find the words?" Margaret asked, coming to stand beside her niece's chair.

Natalie thought it over for a moment, then answered, "I can't seem to settle my mind enough."

"You're nervous about tonight."

It was a statement rather than a question, and Natalie frowned. "Yes, but it's strange. I haven't been nervous before any of the other events Mama has organized for me. Why is this one different?"

Margaret found a comfortable chair for herself nearby and sat down, crossing her ankles and folding her hands in her lap. "Balls always felt different to me than any other kind of gathering," she said, studying her shoes. "You must dance and make conversation and look your best *and* eat or drink without spilling anything on yourself."

"Perhaps that's it," Natalie replied, though she didn't sound convinced.

"For me, going to a ball always made me feel as though I was on display," Margaret continued, noting the small hole in her skirt that would require mending. "Even though there were many other ladies of much higher ranking and greater importance than I was, it always felt as though people were watching me."

She raised her gaze and saw understanding dawn on Natalie's face. "I think that's it. Even though all of the guests tonight are people I have known all my life, I feel as though they will all be watching everything I do."

Margaret offered her niece a sympathetic smile. "Some of them will, particularly in this case because this ball has been organized especially for you. But most people will speak with you, wish you well, and enjoy themselves."

Natalie nodded and was quiet for a moment. Then her eyebrows rose. "When was the last time you went to a ball, Aunt Margaret?"

Margaret's eyes dropped to the hole in her skirt once more. The last time she'd attended a ball, she had already been pregnant with Alex and his father had gone missing. The pitying glances behind fans she'd received that night had only been outnumbered by the disgusted sneers.

"It's been over twenty years now," she replied, hearing the edge in her voice. She shifted in her seat and tried again. "Well before you were born."

"Are *you* nervous for tonight?"

Margaret nodded. "A little."

It was Natalie's turn to smile sympathetically. "Then it's a good thing this is just practice."

And practice Natalie did. Margaret beamed as her niece circulated around the rooms designated for the event in her new white ballgown with tiny flowers embroidered all over, making conversation with her guests with poise and genuine enjoyment that evening. Patrick and Alex, in their best tailcoats and breeches, each danced with her at least three times, and Natalie even got her father to partner her in a country dance.

Margaret made a point of staying away from the action as much as possible, unsure if her presence would be distracting and unwilling to risk ruining Natalie's night to find out. She did dance with her brother and son when they asked, but declined all other offers.

And then Stephen discovered her standing alone in one corner of the drawing room where the refreshments had been laid out.

"Ah, there you are," he said with a wide smile.

She couldn't help but smile back as her heart skipped a beat, and she was glad she'd worn the lilac perfume again that she'd impulsively purchased last month. "Mr. Eddington, are you enjoying your evening?"

"Yes," he replied cheerfully. "I have done nothing but dance and talk and laugh since I arrived, and it's been wonderful. You?"

"It's a lovely party, and Natalie seems to be having fun," Margaret said over the din of the orchestra members tuning their instrument between songs.

"But you're not?"

The question seemed innocent enough, but her smile faltered a bit. "I'm tired, I think."

Stephen nodded. "I suspect I'll fall asleep as soon as my head hits my pillow tonight. I was going to take a walk outside—would you like to join me? Take a break from the noise and the people?"

"That's a lovely idea," she answered before she could stop herself. Philip and Adeleine had strategically placed torches and lanterns in several places outdoors, knowing people would want to do exactly as Stephen was proposing, and Margaret was grateful for the opportunity to get away. She also wanted to speak with him alone, and this was likely her best opportunity to do so.

He followed her lead through the house and offered her his arm when they arrived at the open French windows. She took it, her heart beating rapidly in her chest as she tried to summon the right words to start what would either be a very deep or very awkward conversation. But as they strolled peacefully along in the torchlight, her mind rebelled.

Surely it was permissible to savor this walk in the cool air with a man she cared about. They could talk another day.

"May I ask you an impertinent question?" he asked quietly, as if speaking too loudly would shatter the scenery.

She smiled, recognizing the words she'd spoken to him only a few days ago. "You may."

"Why did you change your mind about attending the house party?" He stopped walking and turned to her. "You could have met Caroline here in your brother's home if that was important to you, or chosen not to meet her at all. But you committed fully to the house party after the note she wrote you."

Her arm slid from his as he clasped his hands behind his back and she missed the contact, even with sleeves and gloves between them. "Two reasons," she said, matching the volume of her voice to his. "First, Caroline said in her note that she doesn't travel often, so this might be our only chance to spend quality time together, and that neither she nor her daughters went about in society so there would be no consequences for them."

The torchlight was dim where they were standing, but the moonlight illuminated his satisfied smile. "And second?"

"I thought it would be a good way to get to know you better." An owl hooted from a distant tree, and she took a moment to gather herself. "Since you are our neighbor and a friend of my brother's, it made sense to spend some time with you to see what kind of person you were outside of a dining room."

He took her gloved hand in his. "And what conclusion did you come to about me?"

She tried to slow her rapid breathing, taking deeper, longer breaths. "That I am fortunate to know you. And that I hope our friendship will continue for many years."

He took her other hand and squeezed it gently. "Did you ever consider that there might be something between us in addition to friendship?"

His voice was husky and the little thrill she felt earlier spread through her body. "I... Yes, I have been thinking a lot about that lately. Have you?"

"Yes," he answered softly, stepping closer. "You are a remarkable woman, Margaret Maitland, and I'm disappointed that I didn't notice sooner."

She knew what was coming next, knew she should stop him, but she didn't want to. Here in this moment, all her worries, all her common sense evaporated in the moonlight. When his arms came around her waist, she slid hers around his neck, combing her fingers through his hair.

His lips found hers, tentatively at first, giving her yet another chance to pull away. But she let her heart lead rather than her head, and deepened the kiss, her body awash in tingly delight when he drew her against him.

She wasn't sure who broke away first, but when their lips parted the merest fraction of an inch, her eyes fluttered open to find him grinning.

"Better than botany books?" she asked with a laugh.

"I want to kiss you while we read your botany books," he replied with an answering chuckle.

She palmed his cheek, then reluctantly drew back. "Perhaps we can try that tomorrow."

"I live in hope," he said, breathing in deeply, audibly, before releasing her with a gusty exhale. "You should probably go back in. I'm going to stay out for a while longer."

She nodded, knowing he was right but unenthusiastic about the idea. "I'm staying here tonight so I can help with the cleanup, but we should find some time together tomorrow—without the botany books," she added, unable to keep the smile from her face.

"We should," he agreed. "Can you come to my study around three o'clock? I'll be working on my correspondence, and we shouldn't be disturbed."

Margaret longed to kiss him again, to hold his warm, solid body against hers, but she stepped away. "Yes, I can manage that."

"Then I will see you tomorrow," he said, kissing the back of her hand before releasing her.

"Tomorrow," she echoed, and dreamily made her way back to the party.

"Stephen, there's a Maitland footman here with a message for you. He says it's urgent."

Caroline's voice broke through Stephen's daydreams. He shook himself back to the reality of lunch with his family as he accepted a piece of paper that was sealed with intertwining M's. That's curious—he and Margaret were going to speak later that day. Why was she sending him a note now? When he broke the seal and read her note, his body ran cold.

Stephen,

Someone saw us, is spreading rumors through the neighborhood. Please come to Eastwood Manor as soon as possible.

Margaret

"Damn," he said quietly, shaking his head.

"Stephen," Caroline scolded. "Watch your language."

He glanced up and noted several of the older children at the table. "Oh, my apologies.

Caroline, is the footman waiting for a response?"

"Yes, I believe so."

"Tell him to hurry back to Eastwood Manor and let them know that I'm on my way."

Caroline gave him a quizzical look. "What's happened?"

He glanced at the children again. "I'll tell you later."

She hurried off to convey the message and Stephen practically ran to his study to finish a letter that needed to be sent off that day. He had a feeling that he'd be spending a large portion of his day at Eastwood Manor and doubted he would see his correspondence again before the morning.

When he arrived at the Maitland home, he was shown into the drawing room by a footman. Stephen wasn't sure what he expected, but Margaret sitting alone in the middle of the room, staring at her hands folded neatly in her lap, was not it.

"Margaret?"

Her chin lifted slowly and her eyes slid to his. "Stephen. I'm sorry to have disrupted your day."

He crossed the room and sat down beside her, reaching out to take her hand. "No apology necessary. This is important."

She placed her bare hand in his and her shoulders relaxed slightly. "One of the guests last night saw us together. I'm not sure how much she saw, but she spent the morning calling on everyone she could get to." Her voice caught and her gaze shifted to his feet. "Apparently that Maitland trollop is up to her old tricks again."

Stephen winced. "Oh, Margaret, I'm so sorry... I should have realized... I didn't even think..."

"I should have known better," she said, her voice barely above a whisper. "I thought because it was a very small event, out in the country..."

"We both thought we were being discreet," he said firmly, leaning down to catch her eye. "Some people simply have to insert themselves into everyone's business."

She met his eyes and held them as he straightened in his chair. "Yes, and being out in the country means she can only contact a limited number of people, so we may be able to mitigate this before it gets out of hand."

"And the easiest way to do that is if we are wed," he said, unable to keep the smile from his face. This isn't the way he would have preferred to start their life together, but he couldn't deny that he was excited by the prospect.

"No, Stephen, that's not what I meant."

"It makes sense, though," he replied, his smile faltering. "And I believe we'll do well together. Even if I wasn't honor bound to do so, I would very likely be asking for your hand in the near future anyway."

"Honor bound?" She withdrew her hand from his and frowned. "Stephen, you can't be honor bound to marry someone who was already ruined."

He studied her face for a long moment. "Margaret, you were born a lady. Through unfortunate circumstances, you weren't allowed to have the marriage—the life—you expected. That doesn't make you less of a lady, less of a *person*."

Her pink lips curved into a smile, but there was only sadness in it. "You are among the few that believe that. My reputation won't change and yours won't suffer if you simply walk away."

"Is that what you want me to do?" he asked in a low voice, afraid the surge of absolute heartbreak would show itself it he spoke any louder. "Is that why you asked me to come here as soon as I could?"

"No," she answered quickly. "No. I thought you should know what was happening. Adeleine has taken Natalie to call on the neighbors that are closest to us, ostensibly to say thank you for attending last night's event, but also to counter these rumors."

"Do you think that will work?"

Margaret shrugged halfheartedly. "Perhaps. If anyone can talk the neighbors round, it's Adeleine. But if she can't, you have options."

"If she can't, my offer stands," he said, covering her hand with his and giving it a gentle squeeze. "I care about you, Margaret, and I meant what I said about asking for your hand anyway."

For a brief moment, her smile radiated warmth and happiness. But it dimmed when she spoke again. "Why don't we both take some time to think things over. I'll stay here today so no one can claim they saw us alone at the dower house, and send you a note with whatever news Adeleine brings when she returns."

He nodded. It was a sensible plan, though every part of him ached to stay. There were consequences for every action, and they both needed to be certain of their decisions. "All right. But if you need me for anything..."

She stood with him and walked him to the drawing room door, touching his arm as they parted. "I will see you tomorrow."

Chapter 7

Margaret looked up as a footman opened the drawing room door to announce Mrs. Gates's arrival. "Caroline?"

Caroline's smile was tentative as she stepped into the room, fine drops of rain clinging to her dress and skin from a brief downpour after Stephen left. "I wasn't sure if you would want to see me."

Margaret rose but was unsure of what else to do. Should she hug her friend? Should she be cautious because Caroline was Stephen's sister? "You are my friend, and I'm always happy to see you."

The two of them found seats in a pair of wing chairs, then sat in awkward silence for several moments until Caroline cleared her throat.

"I wanted to see how you were, if there was anything you needed," she said in a wavering voice.

"I'm well enough," Margaret replied with a genuine smile, "but bored. I was looking forward to playing games with the children today and whatever other activities you had planned."

Caroline sighed. "I was, too. But perhaps we can resume the house party in a day or two."

"Perhaps." Margaret suddenly found her fingernails utterly fascinating, then realized what she was doing. "I'm sorry, Caroline. I feel like I've let you down along with my niece. I didn't mean to ruin your house party."

"First of all," Caroline began, "Stephen has an equal share of the responsibility, so please don't take it all upon yourself."

Margaret stared at her for a moment, then relaxed a bit when she realized Caroline was serious. "Well that's nice to hear for a change."

"And secondly," Caroline continued, her voice lighter, "you didn't ruin anything. We have simply put our shared activities on hold for a while."

"If I agreed to wed your brother, we could pick up where we left off right now," Margaret said. "Did you know he offered for me?"

Caroline nodded slowly. "He told me. He also said that the two of you were taking some time to think things over before making a decision, and that it's best if you aren't staying with us while you do your thinking."

"Yes," Margaret replied, "and I'm glad we have that option. If this had happened in Town, everyone who was anyone would know about our walk under the stars. At least out here everyone is spread out."

"I'm glad, too," Caroline said, leaning against the arm of her chair. "I would love to have you for a sister, but Stephen is a bit impulsive sometimes. It's a good idea for both of you to be very sure about what you want to do."

Margaret inhaled slowly and sighed. "That's what I told him—that we should both be sure. Having me for a wife will not make achieving his ambitions any easier."

"You two can settle that between you," Caroline told her smoothly. Then she shifted in her chair. "If you decide not to wed my brother, will you and I still be friends?"

"I hope so," Margaret said quickly. "I view my friendship with you as separate from my relationship with Stephen, but I would understand if you didn't want to continue it."

Caroline's whole body relaxed. "Oh, I hope we can. I suppose we'll have to wait and see how things turn out between you and Stephen, but I do hope we can still maintain some sort of connection."

Silence fell over them once more and Margaret wondered what on earth they were to talk about after that. Ah, but they didn't need to talk about anything—they could simply have some fun.

"Have you ever played whist with just two people?" she asked, rising and walking to the corner of the room where the bell pull was located.

"How would you even do that?" Caroline said with a giggle. "Whist is for four people."

Margaret grinned. "Normally for four people. Natalie and I got bored one evening when her parents were out and Alex was at university, and we devised a two-handed version. Would you like me to teach you?"

"This I have to see for myself," Caroline laughed.

A footman answered the bell, then went to fetch the deck of cards Margaret requested. While they waited for him, the two women reorganized the furniture in one part of the room so they could play comfortably. When the deck of cards arrived, Margaret seated herself on one side of the table and Caroline on the other.

"For this version of whist, you get twenty cards instead of thirteen..."

Margaret dealt the cards and explained the rules that she and Natalie had invented. They made it through three hands before dissolving into laughter so complete neither of them could continue. When the clock on the mantle struck three, Caroline sighed.

"I'd better be getting back," she said with great reluctance. "I promised I would go with the children to paint this afternoon out in the formal garden if the rain stopped in time, and I can see the sun peeking out through the clouds.

Thank you for allowing Alex to join in today—his presence has been a great comfort to Patrick, and to Stephen, too, I think."

"Whatever happens among us adults, we must make sure that Alex and Patrick feel free to maintain their friendship," Margaret said, standing along with her guest. "Alex has had a difficult time making friends, largely due to the circumstances of his birth. But Patrick, your whole family, never cared. That means a great deal to my son, and to me."

Caroline reached out and hugged Margaret tightly. "I agree. And I hope you and Stephen can come to an amicable understanding, whatever it is."

They said their goodbyes, and Margaret wiped tears from her eyes.

"Was that Caroline Gates I just saw leaving?" her brother asked, entering the room.

Margaret could only nod as another tear dripped down her nose.

"Oh no." Philip enveloped her in his arms, and she breathed in the comforting scent of leather and paper clinging to his clothes. "Did it go poorly between you two?"

Margaret shook her head and managed to croak, "No, we had a wonderful time."

"And that complicates things with Eddington."

She nodded again, grateful to have such a supportive brother. "Caroline is a close friend already, and I'm not sure I could bear to lose her. But I'm not going to wed her brother so I can remain her friend..."

"Of course not," Philip replied gently. "And no one expects you to wed Eddington if you don't want to."

Margaret drew back and wiped her face. "Not even Adeleine?"

"No." When Margaret raised one eyebrow, he continued, "She is worried for our daughter, yes. That's why she's out calling on neighbors now. But neither she nor I think you should marry anyone unless you freely wish to do so."

Her arms went around him again. "You and Adeleine are the reason Alex and I had any sort of life. You know that, don't you?"

She felt Philip's mouth curve against her temple. "I think Cecilia would have swooped in and seen to you and Alex if we hadn't. But we were glad to do so. And we're glad to be of help now, if we can. You know Mama and Papa have their own home—that dower house is yours, always, regardless of your circumstances."

The tears that had slowed started to flow again. How different her life would have been without the support of her family!

When she managed to collect herself once more, she released her brother. "I just don't know what to do, Philip. I feel like it's only these past few weeks that I have really started to know Stephen, and that can't be long enough to fall in love. Can it?"

"You've known Caroline only these past few weeks, and you were just crying over the prospect of not having her as a friend after this," he pointed out.

"Friendship isn't the same as romantic love, though," Margaret replied with a frown. "And it doesn't come with the legal requirements that marriage does."

"I did say the dower house would always be yours," Philip reminded her. "Between Cecilia and me, you never have to worry about how you will live, and neither does Alex."

Her brows crowded down over her eyes. "Are you trying to tell me to marry Stephen and leave him if it turns out we're ill suited?"

Philip shook his head. "I'm telling you that you have the freedom to make the choice you believe is best, and that life is unpredictable but you will always have help when you need it."

She laid a hand on his shoulder and smiled. "You are a good man, Philip Maitland. I am very fortunate to have you as my brother."

"You may change your mind after you hear where I'm going," he quipped.

"You're going to call on Stephen, aren't you?" she countered.

He nodded again. "Not on your behalf. I merely want to see how he's holding up. His closest friend, the person I imagine he'd prefer to talk to right now, is unavailable."

"Ah, yes, Mr. Fitzsimmons and Cecilia are enjoying married life on his farm, according to her last letter," Margaret said with a grin.

"And, apart from his sister, Eddington is on his own."

"Go talk to him, or sit in silence and drink port, or whatever it is he needs to do,"

Margaret said, her smile faltering slightly. "And ask him if we can call on him tomorrow."

"I will."

Margaret stood alone in the drawing room of her brother's home, staring at the door Philip had closed when he departed. The power to decide the direction of her life was in her hands and her hands alone, yet it impacted so many other people.

"What do I do?"

"What do I do?" Stephen asked a stone bust of some ancient Greek figure he'd probably studied at some point during his education.

"Unfortunately, I don't have the answer for you," a familiar voice answered from the door of his study.

"Philip Maitland. You are the last person I expected to see today, unless it was to call me out."

Philip shook his head with a smile. "If my sister were young and impressionable, and you had taken advantage of her, I would. But Margaret passed her fortieth birthday last year

—she is certainly capable of knowing her own mind."

Stephen sat down in his favorite chair and noted that Philip took his customary place on the sofa by the window. "Then why have you come?"

"To see how you are," Philip replied, maintaining easy eye contact. "I know I'm not the best person to talk to in this situation, but with your friend Fitzsimmons otherwise occupied, I thought I might make a passable substitute."

"I appreciate the thought," Stephen told him sincerely. "For I am truly at a loss as to what I should do next. I asked your sister to marry me, did she tell you that?"

"She did."

"She also told me I could just walk away and there would be no consequences," Stephen added, his mouth turning down in a hard frown.

"Oh yes, that sounds like her," Philip said with a chuckle.

Stephen's answering sigh was louder than he'd meant it to be. "So she doesn't want to marry me."

"No, if she didn't want to wed you, she would have said so," Philip explained, clasping his hands together and setting them on top of one knee. "She was simply laying out the facts for you. Because of her already ruined reputation, most of society would not judge you for simply going about your life. You are not, nor will you be, forced into marriage with her."

"Is that true?"

Philip must have heard the skepticism in Stephen's voice, for he leaned forward a little to emphasize his words. "Entirely. Right or wrong, our class puts all the blame on the lady when there is an indiscretion, and most of society still has strong feelings about the birth of her son. You could absolutely go about as if nothing had happened, and her life will stay exactly the same. Yours, too, I imagine."

"Not exactly," Stephen responded, leaning against the arm of his chair. "I'm not sure how I am supposed to go about my life as if I don't care at all for her."

"No outward change in your life, then," Philip amended. "Whatever unresolved feelings you have when this is over, you will have to find a way to cope with."

Stephen rested his chin in his hand. "I certainly will. Have you ever been in a situation like this?"

"Not exactly, but Adeleine did ask for time to think it over when I offered for her."

"She did?"

"Mmhmm. It was excruciating." Philip unlinked his fingers and let his hands drop to his sides. "We were very much in love, but she wanted to be certain that marrying was the right thing for both of us, and that it wouldn't have a negative impact on our families."

Stephen pressed his lips together. "Aren't you supposed to figure that out while you're courting?"

"My wife is a very cautious person, Eddington. She needed to prove to herself that the thing she wanted wasn't going to hurt anyone she loved."

Margaret had that in common with her sister-in-law, though whether it came naturally to her or was a learned behavior after the disappearance of her betrothed, Stephen wasn't sure. "There's sense in that. How long did you have to wait for Mrs. Maitland to answer you?"

"Three days," Philip groaned, lolling his head back against the sofa. "I said it was excruciating. But if Adeleine had asked me to wait a year, I would have. She was—she is—worth it."

"So I should just wait for Margaret to make up her mind?" Stephen asked. Were his feelings not even part of the equation?

Philip sat up. "No. You should know what you want, be ready to explain why you want it. If you have lingering questions, ask them. Margaret usually prefers to come to a decision with anyone else affected rather than imposing her will, so she will want to have a discussion with you. She wants to call here tomorrow, likely for such a discussion."

They discussed various options until they reached a mutually convenient time and Philip stood. "Good. I'll leave you to your thoughts then. Oh, one thing before I depart—whatever happens between you and Margaret is between you and Margaret. Unless you wrong her in some way, you and I can remain on good terms if you wish it."

Philip took his leave and Stephen blew out a breath. "Well, that's something of a relief."

"What is?" Caroline asked, shutting the study door behind her.

"Am I never allowed to talk to myself in this house?" Stephen laughed.

"Not if you plan to live here with someone else," Caroline replied with a grin that immediately turned into a frown. "I'm so sorry, I didn't mean..."

He shook his head and walked her over to the sofa Philip had recently vacated, where they both plopped down rather unceremoniously. "I know."

A companionable silence fell between them until Caroline broke it with a question. "Do you love her, Stephen?"

"I think I have for some time now," he answered softly. "I don't know why, but I didn't see it until just a few days ago. I knew I felt some sort of tenderness for her before that, but then at Miss Natalie's practice ball... That day I just knew."

"What about your ambitions for a high government post?" Caroline asked in a low voice. "From what I understand, you need someone of impeccable lineage and upbringing. The people who judge these things will say

Margaret is lacking morals because of her son, and that will make your climb so much more difficult. Perhaps impossible."

"I believe she's worth it." He didn't say anything else—didn't need to. That one sentence summed up his feelings for Margaret Maitland perfectly.

"Tell her that," Caroline said simply. "Whenever you see her next, tell her that. Then she can make a properly informed decision."

Stephen nodded slowly. "Tomorrow at three o'clock she and her brother are coming to call."

Caroline put her arms around him in a fierce embrace. "No matter what happens between you and Margaret, you will always have my love."

"Even if—"

She cut him off, perhaps not wanting to hear words about a broken friendship spoken aloud. "Even then."

He hugged her back just as tightly. "I know we've had our ups and downs, but you have been a true friend to me as well as a sibling."

She placed a big smacking kiss on his cheek, likely to lighten the mood, and released him. "You have as well, and I'm grateful for it. Try to sleep tonight, and try not to worry about tomorrow."

"I will try," he managed gruffly.

She took her leave but Stephen remained rooted to the sofa. He should answer his pile of correspondence, go through his account books, carry on with all his regular duties and responsibilities. But he needed just another few minutes to himself, to think about what his future would look like with or without Margaret by his side.

Chapter 8

ARGARET KNOCKED ON STEPHEN'S DOOR promptly at three o'clock, glancing nervously at her brother beside her.

Philip offered her a warm smile. "Just follow your heart," he said quietly.

She smiled in return, but hers was less confident. "I'll try."

The butler opened the door and led them to the drawing room where Stephen and Caroline were waiting, Caroline sitting in a chair jiggling one leg, Stephen standing by the fireplace looking outwardly calm except for one hand fidgeting with the chain of his pocket watch.

"Welcome back," Stephen said, crossing the room to meet them at the door. "I hope you don't mind if we dispense with the pleasantries today."

"Not at all," Margaret answered. "Is there someplace we can talk?"

Stephen nodded and gestured toward the door she'd just entered. "Let's go out into the garden."

Margaret glanced back at Philip, who was settling himself in a chair near Caroline looking perfectly content to stay there for a while. "Good idea."

She left the drawing room with Stephen close behind. When he slid his hand into hers and squeezed her fingers, her heard did a little flip. Now that she truly knew this man, could she spend the rest of her lift without him?

When they exited the house, Stephen drew even with her, lacing his fingers with hers as he led her to one of the gardens she hadn't yet spent much time in. It was informally styled, with flowers of every color happily intermingling and an old stone bench set beneath an arbor alive with honeysuckle.

"Would you like to sit?" Stephen asked, nodding in the direction of the bench.

"Probably a good idea," Margaret answered, inhaling deeply as they approached the arbor. "The fragrance of honeysuckle is always stronger at night, but this one smells divine even at this hour."

He grinned. "I hoped you would appreciate it."

She touched his arm with her free hand as they settled onto the bench. What a thoughtful gesture it was to find a place that was both private and appealing to her for what could be a difficult conversation. "I do."

"How did Adeleine fare with the neighbors?" he asked.

"Things went well, from her account," Margaret answered, suppressing the urge to smooth a lock of hair back from his forehead. He'd forgotten to wear a hat and his hair looked rumpled, as though he'd been running his hands through it. "The people she and Natalie visited talked about how much they'd enjoyed the evening, and mentioned that the person attempting to spread rumors was a busybody."

"Oh good," he said brightly.

Margaret continued, "There are likely other guests who are absolutely appalled by our behavior, but they are not Philip and Adeleine's close friends."

"So Adeleine and Philip should escape this incident unscathed."

Margaret nodded. "Natalie, too, though we won't know for sure until she arrives in Town."

They sat together for several long moments in silence that could have easily been uncomfortable, but strangely wasn't, holding hands and enjoying the warmth of the sun. But when the silence stretched on even longer, Margaret began searching for the right words.

Stephen spoke before she could find them. "I am going to ask you a question, and I'd like you to answer as honestly as you can."

"All right."

He clasped both her hands in his and slowly slid his thumbs across them. "If there were no complications, no consequences, would you wish to marry me?"

Straight to the point, then. Well, she could get straight to the point, too. "Yes."

Stephen had been studying their entwined hands, but his eyes darted to hers. "Yes?"

"Yes," Margaret repeated with a light laugh. "I don't wonder at your surprise—I wasn't sure myself until just last night. My affection for you has certainly grown over the past few weeks, and I hope that was obvious at least. But I wasn't convinced that a strong, romantic love could develop between two people in such a short time."

"Until last night," Stephen repeated, squeezing her hands.

"My brother pointed out that I was mightily upset about the prospect of losing Caroline as a friend, and I had known her for only a few weeks. I've known you for the better part of a year and just didn't see it until Philip practically pointed it out to me."

Stephen grinned. "Remind me to send him a bottle of his favorite port."

She laughed again and slid closer to him. "He will be very pleased."

"Does that mean that you love me?" Stephen asked with a slight waver in his voice.

"Yes," she replied, sliding closer to him. "I do love you."

His arms went around her and he pressed his lips to her ear. "I love you, too," he whispered, trailing delicate kisses across her cheek until his mouth met hers.

She twined her arms around his neck and drew him closer, combing her fingers through his hair. But all too soon the sensible voice in the back of her mind reminded her that there were more things to discuss.

Margaret broke the kiss and leaned her forehead against his. "Stephen," she breathed, her eyes fluttering open, "we live in a world where complications and consequences are very real. We can't just run off to Gretna Green because we're in love."

"I know you're right," he murmured, his eyes still closed, "and I'm very glad one of us can be practical when necessary..."

"But?"

His lips captured hers once more. "But I don't want to let you go."

"You don't have to," she replied softly. "We can stay just like this and talk about how to forge our future together."

Stephen grinned. "Excellent. I had an idea last night, also."

Margaret tried to command her heart to slow to a normal pace so she could think, but it refused to obey. She took a deep breath and exhaled slowly, palming his cheek. "What is your idea?"

"You and I will live here and socialize with friends and family," he told her, his grin widening. "We never have to go to London if you don't want to."

"What?" She sat back and let her hands fall to his shoulders. "Stephen, what about your career in government? You must be where they are if you're to have a post."

"I don't need a government post," he said, loosening his arms around her. "It occurred to me last night that it wasn't rank and privilege I wanted, especially if it meant putting you in a distressing position."

Margaret stared at him in disbelief. "What is it that you want, then?"

"Other than you?" he asked with half-smile.

She acknowledged the quip with her own half-smile. "Other than me."

His expression softened. "I want to do some good in this world. In a high enough government position I would have influence and the ear of men with even more influence—I could enact changes in this world for the better." He stroked her back. "But I don't need to be part of the government to change things."

She blinked. "Are you sure? What will you do instead?"

Stephen pulled her closer again. "I'm going to be a country gentleman and a good husband, first and foremost."

"Well that's a relief," she said, not quite able to keep a straight face. "But seriously Stephen, you can't just give up your entire plan for me."

"That's what I realized last night," he said, his grin returning. "I only ever had half a plan —I was going to get myself into a position of influence and 'do good' but it was never more specific than that. Perhaps," he continued, pressing a kiss to her temple, "you can help me figure out the details."

"No plan?" She wanted to simultaneously kiss him and throttle him. She'd been plagued by the notion that her mere presence as his wife would weigh him down like an anchor on a sinking ship. What a relief that they could work together, as partners in life and in occupation! "And you didn't realize this until last night?"

He shook his head. "Something my sister said. When I told her I loved you, she, as you just did, asked how I could reconcile marrying you and climbing the ranks of government."

"What did you tell her?" Margaret asked, tilting her head slightly to one side.

"That you were worth giving up a high ranking position for," he answered in a low voice. "If I had to make the decision one hundred times, I would choose you every single time without hesitation. And that's when I realized that there are other ways to make a difference in the world."

She smoothed his hair back from his forehead. "Remind me to send Caroline a selection of her favorite desserts."

He chuckled. "Our siblings have been rather helpful, haven't they?"

"They're good people," Margaret agreed. "Shall we go tell them the good news?"

Stephen scooped her up and slid her onto his lap. "They can wait a few minutes more..."

Stephen opened the door to the drawing room for Margaret, unable to keep the foolish grin off his face. As soon as they entered, Caroline rose from the chair she'd been sitting in and Philip turned from the painting he'd been studying.

They were both smiling.

"I told you we wouldn't be able to surprise them," Margaret chuckled.

"We don't know the details yet," Caroline said cheerfully, fairly bouncing over to the happy couple.

Philip followed at a more normal pace, but was grinning almost as widely as Stephen. "So we're to have a wedding, then?"

"Yes," Margaret answered, squeezing Stephen's hand. "As soon as the banns can be called."

"I'm going to speak to the vicar tomorrow," Stephen added, glancing at Margaret. His heart swelled so much he thought it might burst, but he contented himself with squeezing her hand back.

"That's wonderful!" Caroline exclaimed, hugging Stephen first, then Margaret.

Philip hugged his sister, then put his arm around Stephen's shoulders. "I'm glad everything worked out for you both."

"She's worth it," Stephen replied quietly.

Philip nodded once, his smile softening, then cleared his throat. "We should celebrate. Eddington, do you have anything special in your wine cellar?"

Stephen summoned the butler and consulted with him for a few moments. "We'll have wine and cake shortly, a footman is on his way to Eastwood Manor to fetch Mrs. Maitland and Miss Natalie, and another is going to find the children. We can have a proper celebration with both families."

"Splendid," Caroline said with a little clap of her hands. "I'm so glad everyone is nearby."

Philip took Margaret aside and Stephen tried valiantly not to listen in. Fortunately, Caroline hugged him again and provided a welcome distraction.

"I'm so glad for you, for both of you," she said with a particularly tight embrace.

Stephen grunted under the pressure of her hug, then grinned. "You'll stay for the wedding, won't you? I know you hadn't planned to be away from your husband for so long."

"Yes, of course I will," she said, releasing him. "Ambrose won't mind spending an extra fortnight or so with his brothers—this is the only time of year when they're able to all be together."

Stephen opened his mouth to reply, but stopped when Patrick entered the drawing room with Alex. Margaret met her son halfway across the room and took his hands. A moment later Alex was grinning.

"Good," Stephen said to his sister.

She waved a hand in front of his eyes. "You only have eyes for your betrothed, don't you?"

"My future stepson has just heard the news," Stephen said softly.

"You should go talk to him," Caroline urged.

Stephen nodded, his gaze lingering on Margaret and Alex. "I will, after he's spoken with his mother."

The siblings talked a bit more, mostly about when Stephen and Margaret might be able to travel to Essex for a visit to Caroline's home, until Alex approached alone. Caroline patted

Stephen's shoulder and went to speak with her own son, taking Stephen's ability to think along with her. There was so much he wanted to say to Alex, but the words just wouldn't come.

"So you and my mother are to be married," Alex said. His voice was even, his posture straight but relaxed...and he was smiling.

Stephen took his cue from the younger man and allowed the grin to return to his face. "We are. I'm sorry I didn't mention the possibility to you sooner."

"Mama and I talked yesterday," Alex replied, shifting his weight from one foot to the other. "I just wanted to say that I'm glad. She's so happy when she's with you, when she talks about you..." He paused again, put his hands in his pockets, then took them out again. "She seems more like herself lately, and I think that's because of you."

"I'll do my best to keep her happy," Stephen managed gruffly. "And you will always be welcome here. In fact, I'm hoping you're still interested in learning how to manage a place like this. You made some good observations when we rode out together, and knowing how to run an estate of any size gives you options when you're ready to forge your own path in the world."

Alex grinned. "So you're going to take on Mama *and* me, are you?"

Stephen chuckled, but then became serious. "The offer is yours to accept or not. Your mother has made her decision about me, but you are your own person and you're certainly old enough to make your own decisions. If estate management doesn't interest you but there's another way I can be of help, all you have to do is ask."

Alex nodded, and just as the conversation was about to turn awkward once again, a footman arrived with the promised wine and cake. The two men joined the rest of their families and helped to pass around plates and glasses.

"Thank you for making time for Alex today," Margaret said, accepting a piece of cake. "I realize that he's old enough now to be wed himself, so it's not as if his life will change much with our marriage. But he's still my son."

"It was my pleasure," Stephen replied—an honest assessment, as he truly did enjoy Alex's company, though hopefully they would become more comfortable with each other again once the newness of the situation wore off. "I told him I would help him in any way I can, though I don't know what the assistance of a builder's son is worth."

She pressed a kiss to his cheek. "It's worth a lot."

Caroline sidled up beside her brother and grinned at Margaret. "Did you tell him yet?"

Margaret's eyes went round. "Oh, not yet—should we wait?"

"No," Stephen cut in with a chuckle, "whatever it is you should tell me now or else it's all I will think about until you do."

"We've come up with a tentative name for this place," Caroline said, between bites of cake. "What do you think of Woodbine Lodge?"

"What is woodbine?" he asked, his eyes shifting from his sister to his betrothed.

Margaret's smile blossomed slowly, dreamily. "Woodbine is an old name for honeysuckle."

Stephen locked eyes with Margaret and his grin matched hers. "Excellent choice."

Caroline bounced away to ask the rest of the guests for their thoughts on Woodbine

Lodge, and Stephen had his betrothed all to himself for the first time since they re-entered the house.

"You're sure about this?" he asked quietly. "It's not too late to go back to the way things were."

"Oh but it is," she replied with a small smile. "Now that I know what it's like to love you, I can never go back to merely being your acquaintance."

He glanced around and, noting that everyone seemed occupied with other things for the moment, dropped a light kiss on Margaret's lips. "Neither could I."

Epilogue

London

June 1816

"**Y**OU'RE SURE ABOUT THIS?" MARGARET asked, the trepidation in her voice evident even to her own ears. The last time she was a guest at a ball, things hadn't exactly gone well. "It's not too late to go back home."

They sat in their carriage, on loan from Margaret's cousin Cecilia, outside a moderately sized townhouse in Brook Street. A friend of a friend had suggested Mr. and Mrs. Eddington as guests to the hosts—Margaret couldn't recall their names now—and after a great deal of thought, they had elected to attend.

"I'm slightly terrified," Stephen answered, taking her hand in his and giving it a squeeze.

They were only in London to see Philip and Adeleine, who were there for Natalie's second season, and a friend of Stephen's from his Cambridge days, who was an MP and in Town for the parliamentary session.

They had no obligation whatsoever to attend this ball.

Margaret looked at her husband in the dim light of the torches held by footmen as they directed carriages and people to their proper locations. He was the most steadfast man she had ever known, defending her when she was maligned by neighbors or merchants, helping her settle into her new life as a wife and mistress of her own life, loving her deeply and fiercely. They'd received this invitation because word of the work he'd been doing at Woodbine was beginning to circulate among the gentry and lower aristocracy.

The least she could do was attend a ball for him.

"Let's go in and see what refreshments they're serving," she said lightly. "If the food is lacking, we'll go home."

He chuckled. "That's the spirit."

When their carriage reached the front of the line, a footman opened the door and let down the steps, assisting Margaret down to the pavement. Stephen hopped out behind her and offered her his arm.

They waited their turn to go through the receiving line and made their way into the area set aside for playing cards. The house was too small for a proper ballroom, but there was enough space for dancing with refreshments set up in an adjoining room, and a string quintet playing a country dance with gusto in one corner.

"Well, there are the refreshments," Stephen quipped, nodding toward a lady carrying a small plate of pastries and a glass of what appeared to be lemonade.

A few guests looked scandalized to see them in public, some turned up their noses, and one lady even yanked the train of her dress to one side when Margaret's gown brushed against it, as if Margaret had some highly contagious disease.

Her chest tightened and her heart began to pound. "Let's see what they have, then, shall we?"

Stephen pressed his lips together and led her through the crowd to the tables laden with pastries and cakes, drinks of all kinds, and even a pineapple placed in the center of the main table on some kind of pedestal.

"Eddington?" a deep voice called.

Margaret and Stephen both turned toward the sound. "Yes?" Stephen answered, scanning the assemblage.

"Eddington!" the voice repeated genially. "I'm glad to have found you in this crush."

"McAlister," Stephen replied warmly to a tall, thin man heading toward them. "I didn't know you'd be here tonight."

"I wasn't going to come," Mr. McAlister confessed, shaking Stephen's outstretched hand, "but when I heard you had accepted I talked myself into it."

Stephen glanced at Margaret, who shrugged. She didn't know this man at all, let alone why he would want to attend an event with her husband.

"I want to introduce you to someone..." Mr. McAlister said, craning his neck to see around the people nearest to them. "Bradford? Bradford! I found Eddington..."

Margaret had let go of Stephen's arm as they made their way through the house, but she reached out and clasped his hand for a moment, giving it a squeeze.

"Mr. Bradford, this is Mr. Eddington, the one who is building the schools in the Cotswolds."

Margaret beamed with pride as the men exchanged pleasantries, then peppered Stephen with questions about his schools. He'd built two so far, with a third one under construction. They were ostensibly for the children of Woodbine's employees and those of the near neighbors, but there were also lessons on Sundays for adults who wanted to learn to read and write. Margaret taught some of the reading classes herself, but the number of pupils had swelled after the first month and other teachers were hired to make sure everyone who wanted to learn could do so.

Margaret squeezed Stephen's hand one more time, giving him a slight nod when he met her gaze, then heading off to circulate on her own. She wasn't particularly excited to do so, but it was one of the unwritten rules of society functions—couples can not spend too much time together, or be too affectionate with each other.

She filled a plate with delicate cakes, nodding to acquaintances who acknowledged her, answering each snide remark with a cheerful smile. She stopped to talk with a friend of Adeleine's who had always treated her like a person worth knowing, and helped two young ladies with the flounces on their gowns. She wandered into the dancing area and leaned against a wall, listening to the string quintet move smoothly from country dance to Scotch reel to waltz.

"May I have this dance, madam?"

She turned, laughing, to find her husband offering her his hand. "I don't feel much like dancing, sir, but would you care for some cake?"

He took a bite of the square she held up for him and closed his eyes. "We need to get the recipe for that one."

"I thought you'd like it," she said, turning to watch the musicians and leaning back against her husband. "How did things go with Mr. McAlister and Mr. Bradford?"

His gloved hand slid down her arm, and his lips brushed against her ear. "Bradford is interested in building a similar school on his estate in Sussex, and he had questions about how we went about building and staffing ours."

"Oh, that's wonderful," she replied, closing her eyes to savor his touch. "I'm sure you had a lot to tell him."

"I did," Stephen said, "but I promised to meet him at his club tomorrow afternoon for a more in depth discussion. I would rather spend this evening with you."

He practically whispered that last sentence and Margaret shivered deliciously. "We have tried the refreshments. Or I have, anyway. Did you want to render an opinion as well?"

"No," he murmured, slipping his arms around her waist. "I trust yours."

"Then let's be off," she replied softly, giving her plate to a passing footman and taking Stephen's hand. They made their way out of the house and into the cool night air, where

Margaret pulled him to a stop. "What shall we do while we wait for the carriage to come round?" she asked, wrapping her arms around his shoulders.

"We could completely scandalize any guests that happen to see us," he suggested, pulling her against him.

"Scandals are what I'm known for," Margaret replied. She managed to keep a straight face just long enough to get the words out, then giggled. "May I kiss you, my love?"

He bent his head to hers and grinned. "Yes, and please be thorough."

His lips were warm on hers, his arms secure around her. In the flickering torchlight, she combed her fingers through his short hair and sighed happily. "Better than botany books."

His laugh was low and gravelly. "Definitely better than botany books."

Ready for more Maitland Maidens? Turn the page to read the first chapter...

When I Fall In Love

Maitland Maidens Book 5

Chapter 1

Kent, August 1816

Sylvie Devereaux sat in her usual place on the brown sofa, lightly rubbing the worn spot on the arm. Her grandparents occupied the wooden chairs on either side of the fireplace, where a small fire burned to try to combat the unusual chill. The low, red light of the evening sun filtering through the windows wasn't quite bright enough to see by anymore, so Sylvie lit the oil lamp on the table beside her, hoping to get some mending done before she went to bed.

Her fingers lingered on the lamp a moment, the smooth metal cool to the touch for a few moments before it began to warm. This particular lamp had been a rather costly wedding gift to her grandparents from both their families, the result of a numerous relatives pooling what they could spare to purchase something truly beautiful…and useful. Sylvie's grandparents had brought it with them when they emigrated from France, a symbol of the family they left behind and the hope they cherished for their future.

Was this the future they had envisioned?

"How does the field look, Grandpère?"

It was a topic they had discussed at least once each day during the growing season, usually in this fashion around the fireplace or while they ate supper, for as long as Sylvie could remember. Grandpère would inevitably talk about the height of the wheat, the color and strength of the stalks, or a myriad of other tiny but important details that signaled the health of their crop.

But this season had been different. This *weather* had been different.

His silence stretched out so long that Sylvie put down her needle and looked up at her grandfather. His eyes had met his wife's, his mouth turned down into a hard frown that didn't ease when he finally answered.

"Not good, ma chérie. We may not have much of a crop this year."

Not a surprise and yet wholly surprising all at the same time. Sylvie had been half-expecting this bit of news for the past several weeks now, but to hear her grandfather say it aloud was like a physical blow to her chest.

"Still too wet," her grandmother added, returning to her own sewing. "The kitchen garden has been struggling all summer, too."

Sylvie had noted the lack of production in the kitchen garden herself, trying to find enough produce to eat with each meal. There was never enough, and what was growing was undersized and slow to ripen.

Grandpère nodded. "And too cold. Wheat doesn't like a great deal of heat, but it needs some warmth."

"And sun." Sylvie pressed her lips together, recalling the abnormally high number of dark, rainy days they'd had this year. Even this day they'd only seen a bit of sun as it set, and that was more than most. "Do you think we'll be able to pay rent this quarter?"

The fire gave a loud pop and sent out a plume of thick smoke as he sighed heavily. "For the first time since you were a little girl, I don't know. If we get enough sun in the next few weeks, there may be something to harvest. But if the rain keeps falling..."

He didn't have to finish his sentence. If the rain kept falling, any wheat that had managed to grow in their field despite the conditions would rot at the root and there would be no harvest. Sylvie also didn't need to ask if he'd thought of borrowing money—her parents might have a little to spare, but likely not enough to cover rent for the farm. And they were in France with no way to send money or to return to England themselves. A bank loan might be a possibility, but without a crop to use as assurance...

"Try not to worry," Grandmère said, turning in her chair to meet Sylvie's gaze, her face partially cloaked in shadows. "There is still time to figure something out."

There was a measure of comfort in her words, but Sylvie was too practical to be swayed very much by them. If Grandpère said things were looking dismal, then there was reason to worry.

"There are always my animals."

In addition to the three people and the wheat fields, the farm housed a flock of geese, a few goats, some laying hens, and a dairy cow, all of whom would need to be fed through the winter. They weren't truly hers, but Sylvie had taken over caring for the farm's livestock as an adolescent and had hand raised many of the goats and geese herself. As a result, Grandpère had taken to calling them hers.

He raised a hand to object, but she held up her own to stop him. "Not Moses, of course." She suppressed a shudder at the thought of sending her special pet, a goose that she'd raised from an abandoned egg, off to someone's dinner table. "But the others should fetch a good price. That is why we keep them, and if it means keeping our home..."

Grandmère sent her a sympathetic look, then sighed herself. "Hopefully it won't come to that."

"But if we need to," Sylvie continued, turning their alternatives over in her mind, "it wouldn't be that different from other years. We've sold animals before."

"Yes, when we run out of room for them," Grandpère answered gruffly. "I will go to

London and talk to his lordship myself before we sell off your entire collection."

Sylvie was certain Grandpère wouldn't even know what their landlord, the Marquess of Whitby, looked like, let alone find the wherewithal to go and speak to the man, but she kept that to herself. She also noted the red creeping into Grandpère's cheeks that couldn't all be attributed to the fire and turned the conversation to a new topic. "Perhaps I can take in some mending, then, or do some cooking for the neighbors. Mr. Mathison next door is a bachelor, and so is Mr. Ross across the way—I could speak to them both tomorrow."

Grandpère nodded, his face returning to its normal color. "I suppose it wouldn't hurt to inquire. And if we do end up with enough wheat to pay the rent, you'll have a little money put by for your future."

Her future. Sylvie suppressed a shiver and tried to focus on her needle going in and out of the soft, worn fabric of her second best dress. When Grandpère died, her father would likely be allowed to take over the copyhold on the farm if he chose to, but there was no telling when he and her mother would return, or if they'd even want to take up farming again. What if they decided to stay in France? They had a comfortable home there now with her mother's parents. What was there to come back to here except unending hard work and rain?

Sylvie gave up on her mending and said goodnight to her grandparents, trudging slowly up the stairs to the bedchamber she'd occupied all her life. How much longer would it be hers?

What would she do when it wasn't?

Cold water dripped onto Kit Mathison's face, which was occasionally accompanied by a chilly breeze. He blinked his eyes open but quickly squeezed them shut again, pulling the blanket up over his face to block out the small deluge. But instead of soft, dry blanket, he was met with sopping fabric that threatened to drown him before he could rise from his bed.

"Thomas, you've left the tent flap open again," he said with a yawn, his eyes still tightly shut to keep the water out of them. "It must have rained last night."

He felt about for a patch of dry cloth to wipe his face with and found part of his nightshirt that was unaffected. Rolling over onto his side, he pushed the blanket off and struggled to a sitting position as the dripping continued to wet his hair and clothes. "Thomas?"

Kit opened his eyes to find that he was not, in fact, in a tent behind the house with his younger brother, as his sleep-addled mind had believed, but alone in the big bed in the master's chamber.

"What the devil is going on?"

Another cold stream landed in his lap and he leaped out of bed. What the devil *was* going on? He held his hands out, palms up, eyes wide as he looked around the room.

Yes, it was definitely raining inside the house.

His house.

And there was a very large hole in *his* roof.

He stood in the corner of the room for a moment, unmoving except to blink, staring dumbly at the raindrops falling through the ceiling. How did this happen?

How much would it cost to repair?

Kit shook himself and set about dressing in dry clothes, thankful that the rain hadn't damaged his wardrobe...yet. He made his way down the stairs and stopped in the kitchen to butter a piece of bread, shifting the bread from one hand to the other as he put on his old, patched tailcoat and hat.

"All right, let's see how bad it is."

The rain had abated and the bread was reduced to crumbs by the time Kit stepped out the front door. He managed to wrestle the tall ladder and a large tarpaulin out of the barn with the help of one of the stable lads and hauled them one at a time to the house. When the two of them had propped the ladder against the house as close as they could to Kit's bedchamber, Kit climbed resolutely to the top with a rope tied to the tarpaulin while the stable lad held the bottom of the ladder steady. The ladder was just tall enough to reach the second story of the house, forcing Kit to scramble up onto the roof to survey the damage.

"How does it look?" the stable lad called?

Kit stayed low, crawling from the edge of the roof toward the hole, his eyes growing wider as he drew nearer.

"Oh no."

A large portion of the roof had collapsed into the attic space some time ago, judging by the weathering of the timbers poking out. And each time rain fell from the sky during this very wet summer, it had collected in the newly bared attic—he could see the water stains on the attic floor—weakening the structure.

The rain that morning was merely falling through a ceiling that had been rotting away for weeks.

Kit sighed wearily. "How could I have missed this?"

He spent a few more minutes surveying the damage, then pulled the tarpaulin up to the roof and secured it over the gaping hole, trying to commit the details of the damage to memory so he could make a sketch later. A careful check of the other parts of the roof he could reach yielded even more information—three other places where shingles were loose or damaged, and water was likely already getting in.

When Kit reached the ground again, his stable lad wasn't the only one waiting for him.

"Moses! Have you come to swim in my bedchamber?"

The big white bird looked up at Kit and turned sideways, asking to be scratched the way Kit's childhood dog had done once upon a time. Both Kit and the stable lad obliged before hefting the ladder once again and hauling it back to the barn, with Moses waddling alongside them.

Once the ladder was stowed, the stable lad went back to his usual work and Kit headed back to the house, walking slowly around the perimeter looking for other issues.

"The roof was damaged, you see," Kit explained to the goose as they circled the house, "and I didn't realize it until just today. It's made a terrible mess inside the house, and I fear it's going to take a long time to restore."

A gust of wind blew through, ruffling Moses's feathers. He resettled his wings with a little shake.

"Indeed."

With another sigh, Kit made note of a couple of places under the eaves that were showing early signs of water damage. "Do you want to come in while I write these all down? Or shall I walk you home first?"

The first few times Kit had met Moses, he'd felt rather silly talking to an animal that most people would make into Christmas dinner. But the bird's owner, Kit's neighbor, had insisted that Moses had a personality and enjoyed conversation, and Moses had begun wandering over to Kit's farm on his own from time to time.

Apparently he liked the company here. And the stream that ran across one corner of the property. And the scratches. But he never seemed to be able to find his way back without a human escort.

Moses looked around, then met Kit's eyes and huffed a sigh.

"Home it is then, lad."

Kit started off toward Broadstone Farm, the home of Mr. and Mrs. Devereaux and their granddaughter, with Moses waddling along beside him.

Other Books by Cora Lee

Sweet & Traditional:
Save the Last Dance for Me (Maitland Maidens #1)
Back In My Arms Again (Maitland Maidens #2)
Kissing by the Mistletoe (Maitland Maidens #3)
A Kiss to Build a Dream On (Maitland Maidens #4)
When I Fall In Love (Maitland Maidens #5)

Spicy Novellas:
What If I Loved You

Spicy and Suspenseful:
No Rest for the Wicked
The Good, The Bad, And The Scandalous
The Duke of Darkness

About The Author

Cora Lee is National Bestselling author of Regency romance. She went on a twelve year expedition through the blackboard jungle as a high school math teacher before publishing *Save the Last Dance for Me*, the first book in the Maitland Maidens series. She then followed it up with eight more novels and novellas, ranging from sweet and traditional to spicy and suspenseful.

When she's not walking Rotten Row at the fashionable hour or attending the entertainments of the Season, you might find her participating in Regency Fiction Writers events, wading through her towering TBR pile, or eagerly awaiting the next Marvel movie release. If you'd like to find out more about Cora or her books you can visit her website, sign up for her newsletter, or connect with her on Bookbub, Facebook, or Goodreads.

www.ingramcontent.com/pod-product-compliance
Lightning Source LLC
Chambersburg PA
CBHW032014180726
48283CB00008B/2668